The Other Side

Joan Calmady-Hamlyn

Pen Press

First published in Great Britain by
Pen Press
25 Eastern Place
Brighton
BN2 1GJ

ISBN13: 978-1-906710-67-5

Printed and bound in the UK

A catalogue record of this book is available from
the British Library

Cover design by Jacqueline Abromeit

1

There was nothing to indicate that the two men, conversing quietly at a corner table in a Hamburg café, were both Commanders in their respective navies. They were in their early thirties and soberly suited in grey but Henry Parkin USN wore a neat, spotted bow tie and Henry Hillman RN sported a striped Service tie.

There was no doubt, however, about the three young men just entering the café. They all wore long naval greatcoats with lieutenants' insignia on the shoulder straps and peaked caps with the eagle and swastika riding aggressively over the naval badge.

The two Henrys, whose ships were making courtesy calls, watched the new arrivals, thoughtfully. It was December, 1938 and there seemed little doubt now that Britain and Germany would soon be at war and young men such as these would be the foe.

'See the first one, Harry?' said Hank Parkin. 'He came aboard with his CO and Number One last night. Dinner in the Wardroom. In the course of conversation I understood his CO to call him a fine officer and the Number One to call him a bloody swine – or words to that effect.'

Commander Henry Hillman took a sip of wine. The man in question had stripped off his gloves and removed his cap to show fair hair and superciliously gazing blue eyes. The Herr Ober, greeting the three effusively, led them to a table not far distant.

'Name's Reissenburg,' continued Parkin, lighting a cheroot and signalling to the waiter for coffee. 'Father's an Admiral or was – has a bloody great estate somewhere north of Hanover.'

'Admiral von Reissenburg was with the Imperial Fleet in the Great war,' said Hillman. 'And retired. If his son's a Nazi I shouldn't think it makes for a smooth relationship.'

Parkin grinned.

'The Armed Forces don't belong to political parties,' he pointed out. 'You getting home for Christmas, Harry? Is it true the Nazis have rewritten the words to carols and cut out all religious references? Should have thought it 'ud just be easier to ban them altogether.'

Hillman smiled. He finished his wine as the waiter brought coffee.

'The Germans are a sentimental lot,' he said. 'I can't see them giving up their carols at their Christmases. Hamburg's our last call so, with any luck, I should be home for Christmas. Will you make it?'

'We're off tomorrow. Five days if the Atlantic's kind. Yeah – should just do it. Now, are we going to have a look at the Reeperbahn?'

'If we must. I warn you I shall not be enticed! But, at least, you'll be able to say you've been there.'

'Yeah. If I were ten years younger – like those over there – I might be tempted.'

They stood up and took their overcoats and hats from the coat-stand by the table.

The movement attracted the lazy gaze of Leutnant von Reissenburg who evidently recognized the American Commander from his visit to the US ship. He stood up and made a short, stiff bow, unsmiling, which Parkin acknowledged with a navy salute. He and Hillman went out.

Their wild oats had been sown as snotties, subs and lieutenants. A more sophisticated view of life came with the half-stripe and now the pornographic temptations of the Reeperbahn roused little more than naïve shock on the part of the American and cynical revulsion in the Briton. They took a cab to the docks and parted to gain their respective ships.

The US cruiser duly sailed the following morning and a couple of days later, Commander Hillman RN, having searched the Hamburg shops for Christmas presents to take home to his family, went into the same café to revive himself with lunch. He had just ordered when a man in uniform came up to the table. He removed his cap as he approached and Henry recognized the lazily dissolute-looking Leutnant Reissenburg.

'Will you permit me to sit here?' he said in heavily accented English.

Henry glanced around. The café was by no means full.

'If you wish, Leutnant von Reissenburg,' he said.

The man hung his greatcoat and cap on the stand and sat down.

'Thank you,' he said. 'Usually I drop the "von".'

'But your father remains von Reissenburg – a distinguished Admiral.'

Reissenburg glanced at the menu and threw a curt order at the waiter.

'That is so,' he said. 'But I doubt if they will name a ship after him – like the *Graf Spee*, *Admiral von Scheer* and *Tirpitz*.'

'*Tirpitz*?' repeated Henry. 'Is that the one after *Bismarck*?'

'The *Bismarck* is launched in two months. Then *Tirpitz*.' Reissenburg paused as the waiter put a plate before him. Henry found himself slightly surprised to see it was a relatively simple dish; he could visualize Reissenburg wallowing in the fleshpots. The lazy eyes watched him. 'Then we go to war, h'n?'

Henry chewed thoughtfully on his mouthful.

'Is that what you expect?' he said, when he had finished.

'It is what I fear.'

'You don't want war? Why?'

'Because we cannot win. That little gutter-rat will lead us to defeat and destruction again – to another Scapa Flow, another Versailles. We are just back on our feet now. Lebensraum! Why do you think he goes east?'

'Oil,' said Henry.

'Yes. We have no oil. Without it he cannot fight his war.' Reissenburg lifted a hand and the waiter came scurrying. He ordered coffee and cognac and looked at Henry. 'Will you also, please?'

'Yes. Thank you.' Henry waited until the waiter had gone then he said, 'Why do you tell me all this?'

Reissenburg shrugged. 'It will be in your mind that we do not all want war with you.' The coffee and cognac came and he looked down at Henry's parcels. 'You have gifts for your family? For children?'

Henry accepted the change of subject.

'Yes. I have parents, sisters, a wife and two children. You? No, you're too young.'

Reissenburg drank coffee, broodingly. 'I have parents and a young brother.'

'Hitler Youth?'

'No! No, my father would not allow. He will be a naval cadet.'

Henry considered him. Immaculately uniformed. A fine officer and a bloody swine. Henry felt both descriptions could probably apply. The man raised his glass of cognac.

'To the British Navy,' he said, with a sudden smile and tossed it back. Henry, startled, honoured the toast and Reissenburg got to his feet. 'I must go now, Commander. Thank you for allowing me to talk to you.' He pulled on his greatcoat, took his cap and bowed to Henry. Then he went.

Henry drank his coffee, wonderingly. So the man knew he was a naval officer – senior to himself, cheeky bastard – and what could be the meaning of his talk? Did he want it passed on to somebody in a position of authority? Was it a veiled suggestion that something should be done to stop 'that little gutter-rat' before he went any further?

The waiter came up and put his bill on the table. It was stamped as 'Paid'. Arrogant young bugger! Henry put on his overcoat and hat and collected his parcels. At least he was more or less prepared for Christmas.

The British cruiser set sail the following day, their round of civic and military visits duly accomplished and their hosts entertained aboard in return. A German destroyer courteously escorted them down the Elbe and waved a metaphorical goodbye off Cuxhaven. Henry focused his glasses on the bridge and without surprise found the Leutnant z.S. Reissenburg standing on the wing, watching them. He raised a hand to the salute and disappeared into the wheelhouse.

'Got a friend aboard, Henry?' asked Captain Bateson's voice at his shoulder.

'An acquaintance, rather,' said Henry. 'It's an odd story.'

Bateson viewed the group on his bridge, all experienced hands.

'It's plain sailing from here,' he said. 'We'll leave it to the OOW. Come below and tell me.'

In Bateson's fore-cabin, over a mid-morning glass of Madeira, Henry recounted his two meetings with the German junior officer. Bateson mulled it over for some minutes.

'Then he toasted the British Navy and thanked you for letting him talk to you?'

'Yes, sir.'

'I can't seriously believe that the German Navy is planning to mutiny – before a war starts – as they did at the end of the Great War – can you?'

'No, sir. Is it that they hope for more diplomatic activity to avert war?'

'Could be. I'm to see the Commander-in-Chief when we get in. I'll pass it on to him and we'll see if he thinks it worth taking higher.'

The ship was based at Devonport and Henry got to his comfortable four-bed roomed semi-detached at Yelverton on Christmas Eve. His parents lived on the edge of Dartmoor, near Tavistock, with one of his sisters still at home. They were entertaining the married sister and her family this Christmas so

Henry, his wife Jean and the two children, Toby and Anne, were celebrating as a small family this year. Thank the Lord; thought Henry, for Christmas in an extended family now there were four youngsters varying from two years to eight was a bit too much for him. Apart from a visit to Tavistock, he would be able to spend a nice peaceful week at home.

2

Leutnant zur See Manfred von Reissenburg – who usually dropped the 'von' – also got home on Christmas Eve. It was their time for celebration and the exchanging of gifts, something Hitler had not managed to abolish and he greeted his mother with a formal kiss on each cheek as she smiled approvingly at the immaculate uniform with the ten shining buttons, the two gold stripes and star on the sleeves. In front of the great stone hearth with its blazing log fire, the Admiral-Graf stood, feet apart as on his quarter-deck, thin, grey-haired, and austere. Totally unabashed, sixteen-year-old Baldur sat hugging his knees on the thick rug on the floor by the tall Christmas tree, grinning a welcome to his older brother.

Ignoring him, Reissenburg approached his father, snapped his heels together and ducked his head, briefly. The Admiral observed him, impassively.

'Good evening, Manfred,' he said. 'You have time to change before dinner.'

'Thank you, my father.' He went from the hall.

'Go, too, Baldur,' said the Grafin and the boy jumped up and chased after his brother.

'I suppose we cannot hope for more than that he serves the Navy well and does not disgrace his family,' sighed the Admiral.

'He will come with us, tomorrow?' said the Grafin.

Christmas dinner was a formal occasion with five courses served and wine in abundance. Baldur plied his brother with questions on the Navy which he was shortly to join.

'We have some splendid ships now that we have been allowed to build. We must be near to the British Navy now –

Scharnhorst and *Gneisenau, Deutschland, Graf Spee* – and *Bismarck* to come.'

'All to skulk in harbour like the High Seas Fleet after Skagerrak,' said Reissenburg, scathingly.

'There were no more sea battles after 1916,' said the Admiral, sharply, 'because the British Grand Fleet did not come out again.'

'Must we talk of this at Christmas?' asked the Grafin.

'Don't talk of Christmas to Manfred,' chuckled Baldur. 'You're a pagan, aren't you, Manny? Is it Siegfried or Wotan?'

'The boy needs curbing,' said Reissenburg, coldly. However, he respected his mother enough to ask her of the affairs of Reissdorf whose cottages clustered around them and his father of the machine works at Reissbaden which made marine engines and components and was owned by the family. Baldur fell silent, fairly certain that his use of the name 'Manny' had earned retribution which would come in due course. He knew something of his brother's reputation for harsh efficiency and vowed that he would be as efficient a naval officer but a popular one. He applied himself to his dinner with renewed vigour.

The giving and receiving of presents took place after dinner and, that completed, Reissenburg excused himself, pleading weariness after the journey from Hamburg. He made his way up the broad staircase to his own apartments, which consisted of sitting-room, bedroom and bathroom. Pyjamas and dressing-gown had been laid out on the thick, down coverlet of the tall, carved four-poster and slippers side by side on the floor. He rejected the idea of ringing for the servant who valeted him when at home and stripped off his evening suit, starched shirt and wing collar. When changed he went into the sitting-room where a log fire blazed and a tray of drinks was on a side-table. He poured himself a whisky, flicked on the wireless and sat down in an armchair. The radio station was playing Wagner, a performance of 'The Ring'. Baldur's voice teased his mind. He did not bother to change the station: the fierce stridency of the music and the singing suited his mood. He wondered if the English Commander had understood what had prompted him to talk as he had. He envied and admired the Royal Navy which he had come up against in various parts of the world, including a never-to-forgotten courtesy call at Colombo the previous year and he did not want to meet them in battle. But no-one, it seemed, would stop Hitler dragging the country headlong to disaster. Even his father could only speak of how the shame of Versailles had been wiped out.

The sitting-room door opened and his father came in, spare, upright, commanding. He got up and turned off the wireless.

'You could not spare your mother any more of your time?'

'I am sorry.'

'For this evening I should have expected you to overcome your travel fatigue. We see little of you. You will attend the church service in the morning.'

'I was going to ride –'

'You will attend the church service in the morning.'

'Yes, my father.'

'Your mother wishes it. Good night, Manfred.'

The Admiral left the room and the lieutenant savagely poured himself another stiff whisky.

In Yelverton, Toby and Ann were in bed, whether or not asleep Henry had yet to find out. He and Jean were busily wrapping up small parcels and stuffing them into Christmas stockings. When they were stuffed as full as they would go, he reached out for the champagne bottle and refilled their glasses.

'Got the sherry and mince pie ready for Santa?' he asked.

She curled up against him, contentedly, the fairy lights on the tree reflecting with the firelight in her eyes.

'I'm glad you got home for Christmas this year,' she said. 'I suppose it could be the last Christmas of peace.'

'If we can't stop Hitler invading Poland, yes. We dare not let him get away with any more.'

'Oh, dear.' She sat up, cross-legged and took a drink. 'We'll forget about it for this week. When do you go back?'

'New Year's Eve. We sail the following week.' The clock struck midnight and Henry raised his glass. 'Happy Christmas, darling.'

'And may we have many more. Let's see if the kids are asleep and hang up their stockings.'

But stockings were only the beginning of Christmas and there were the gifts under the tree, the Christmas turkey or goose and the pudding and mince pies – for the lucky ones – and possibly the visits to or from relations for tea and Christmas cake and more crackers. All over England families were celebrating some form of Christmas, some of them conscious that it was likely to be the last one at peace, some of them quite happy in the conviction that Chamberlain's 'piece of paper' guaranteed 'peace in our time.'

In Germany, the Christmas Eve festivities over, those who did not follow the Nazis' rejection of Christian teaching, went to their Lutheran or Catholic churches for the morning service on Christmas Day and sang carols to welcome the Christ Child and praise his Virgin Mother.

In Reissdorf, the Reissenburg family attended the village church. They had their own chapel but accepted that the Pastor had no time for an extra service on Christmas Day and, in any case, it was expected that they join the villagers for all religious festivals. To have both the sons this year was a bonus for of late the elder had been either at the Naval Academy or at sea and the younger would soon be off as a cadet, too. The first months, of course, were done as an ordinary seaman with scrubbing the decks and cleaning the heads and all that, and how was the lively young Baldur going to knuckle down to that? Leutnant Manfred had done it but he was a different kettle of fish entirely with his rigid self-discipline and strong sense of duty.

So 1939 crept into being and some eight days later Henry's ship sailed for the Falklands and on the same day Manfred

Reissenburg's destroyer set sail as escort to the Admiral Group West's flagship en route for Argentina and port visits to Buenos Aires and others along the coast. But they were some hundreds of sea miles behind HMS *Billericay*, the cruiser commanded by Captain Bateson whose Executive Officer was Commander Henry Hillman.

For all the ease and comforts of his home, Reissenburg was happy to be at sea again. His habit of command and also of obedience came from his ancestry. His excellence as an officer came from his interest in the handling of a ship and, also, perhaps, because he put duty first. If his handling of men could be somewhat harsh, he was very disciplined himself and did not expect less from others. He looked forward to the challenge of the Atlantic and to reaching warmer seas. It crossed his mind as they entered the Dover Strait that this route to the Atlantic would be barred to them in the event of war. Surely Hitler could not be so mad as to invite war with England again. And America? The fine ship, the SS *Bremen* was sailing to New York, carrying passengers hoping to settle there, escaping from the Nazis. But Hitler had barred any more Jews from leaving the country. Why? If he wished to be rid of Jews, let them go. Most of the Jew shops in Hamburg were empty and boarded up now, anyway. He only knew of a couple of Jew families in Reissbaden. Would they be got rid of, too? He bent to a voice pipe and gave a correction of course. The Coxswain on the wheel repeated it back.

They were keeping well out into the Channel though the Cs-in-C of both Portsmouth and Plymouth knew of their passage. If they were still at peace on their return, they would probably make port calls. If not... they would be making their return via the Denmark Strait no doubt.

He bent to the voice pipe again.

'Keep station on the flagship – you're all over the place.'

'Aye, aye, sir,' said the Cox'n and added to himself, 'If only the bleeding flagship kept steady.'

The German ships reached the Argentine port some day-and-a-half after HMS *Billericay* had anchored off Stanley. The British cruiser then proceeded a thousand miles to George-Town in British Guiana. It was here that the two German vessels caught up.

Henry, descending Billericay's brow, already uncomfortably hot in his white uniform, saw the smart picket-boat from the German destroyer arrive at the jetty steps and recognized the also-white-clad lieutenant who disembarked first.

'Ah – von Reissenburg,' he said as the man reached the top of the steps. Reissenburg snapped to the salute and Henry smilingly returned it.

'I owe you a lunch,' he said. 'Are you off sightseeing or will you join me now?'

'If you know of somewhere shady that serves long, cool drinks, I will join you now, Commander – and thank you.'

Shady as in shade, mused Henry or shady as in – whatever. Reissenburg probably would not know that meaning of the word, anyway. They strolled along the glaringly bright streets among the highly-coloured goods displayed for sale until they came upon a likely-looking place which offered shaded tables and black, happily smiling waiters in multi-coloured shirts and spotless white trousers. From it, they could see the German cruiser and her destroyer screen anchored off shore, white paint gleaming in the relentless sun. Billericay, moored to the quayside, was not in view.

'We do not have the opportunities you have to come to exotic places,' said Reissenburg. 'So, whenever we do, I come ashore, even if to get only so far.'

'It will be hot aboard,' said Henry, peacefully. 'Did you have a good Christmas?'

3

On her return to Hamburg, the destroyer in which Leutnant z.S. Reissenburg served was paid off and he went home on a month's leave. Towards the end of May he was instructed to report to Berlin in civilian clothes. The weather was fine so he chose a light-weight grey suit, took an overnight bag and caught the train from Hannover. What lay ahead he could not imagine but he presumed there would be the opportunity to return home for more clothes, uniforms or whatever was needed before proceeding on the next posting. The address in Berlin where he was to report was unknown to him and first forebodings came to him when he realised it housed the Abwehr, the office of Counter-Intelligence.

He was taken to a room bleakly furnished with filing cabinets and a large desk at which sat a man in the uniform of an Army Major. There was no name on the door and the Major did not identify himself. He waved Reissenburg to a chair on the opposite side of the desk.

'You lunched with a British naval commander just before Christmas,' he said.

'Yes.'

'And again with the same man in Georgetown.'

'By chance, entirely.'

'What was the gist of your conversation with him, do you recall?'

Reissenburg stared, perplexed.

'No – trivia, only.' About Christmas, about cruisers, about – oh, God!

'It is trivia to refer to our Fuhrer in derogatory terms and to infer he leads to defeat and destruction?'

'I wanted to get a British reaction to such statements.'

'And did you?'

'He understood that the Fuhrer seeks for oil in his expansion eastwards.'

'As a naval officer you have sworn personal allegiance to Adolph Hitler?'

'Yes, of course. What is it you want of me?'

The Major leaned back in his chair, joining his finger-tips.

'In view of those very unfortunate remarks of yours, you will have to prove that allegiance. You will go to England. As of this moment, you are missing, presumed dead. You will be contacted when you get to England and told of your mission. If you do not carry it out, your parents will receive confirmation of your death. If you do well, we may be able to resurrect you as a hero of the Reich. Now you will be taken and prepared for your journey. Heil Hitler.'

Reissenburg did not reply and was taken out to a car by an Army corporal. His mind was reeling. England? But – the Navy, his career? He, who was to be an Admiral like his father, he, whose reports all called him a brilliant officer, who was due for promotion. Missing, presumed dead. Would his parents, his colleagues, think he had defected, run for it? And what had he to do in order to be 'resurrected'?

The car stopped at what he recognized as the SS headquarters and he went with his escort to the office of Colonel SS Kranz.

Kranz, a tall man who set off his uniform well, regarded his captive.

'What is this? What is happening?' demanded Reissenburg. 'I'm a naval officer –'

'No,' said Kranz softly. 'Leutnant Reissenburg is dead. You are Max Reiss, a marine engineer, escaping to England from the tyranny from the Nazis.'

Reissenburg rubbed the back of his hand across his mouth. This was a nightmare, this could not be happening.

'Please, Colonel,' he said. 'I do not understand what is wanted of me.'

'You will,' said Kranz, pleasantly. 'You are here so we may teach you. Now, what is your name?'

'Manfred von –'

'What is your name?' The words were harsh, threatening.

Reissenburg felt cold sweat on his face.

'Max Reiss,' he said, faintly and let darkness enfold him.

Through a haze he felt himself being half-lifted, half-dragged along a corridor and into a small room. There he was pitched on to a hard narrow bed and lay stunned, unbelieving, desperate, helpless.

He must have drifted into a half-sleep, half-stupor from which he was sharply awakened when the door was flung open and a voice shouted 'Attention! What is your name?'

He stumbled to his feet.

'Manfred von –'

He received a blow across the face.

'What is your name?'

'Max Reiss.'

'Where are you from?'

They had not told him the answer to that one.

'Reissdorf?'

Colonel Kranz strolled into the room. He was smoking an Egyptian cigarette in a long holder.

'So you still have some wits about you, Reiss? Yes, you come from Reissdorf. You are one of the family by-blows and you work in the engineering firm making marine engines. Understood?'

Reissenburg struggled to imagine his correct and frigid father distributing illegitimate offspring amongst the peasantry of Reissdorf. It was a well-known belief of the town bourgeoisie that the country landlords did this.

'Understood, Colonel,' he said.

'Take off your clothes. All evidence of your identity must be removed.'

'Hand-me-downs – from the family,' murmured Reissenburg, sarcastically.

Kranz made an exasperated gesture and the SS man who had entered first dealt Reissenburg another blow across the face. He removed his shoes and socks, all marked for the navy, his suit with his name on the tailor's label, his shirt and tie also marked. His undershorts, unmarked, he retained. The SS man checked the waistband, gathered up the rest and followed Kranz from the room.

In the morning, some of the shock of his situation had worn off. He met the arrival of Kranz and his under-officer, ready to question.

'Colonel, where is the authorization from the Navy that I am to be sent to England?'

Kranz contemplated him. A slim, straight, well-muscled torso, clad only in the white shorts.

'There is no authorization. Leutnant Reissenburg is missing, presumed dead.' He smiled. 'Was it your dislike of the Nazi regime that caused you to desert? Your contempt for the Fuhrer? Your fear of another war?'

'I am no coward,' he retorted, fiercely.

'Will your father, the Admiral, believe that?'

Horrified, Reissenburg cried out, 'You can't do this – you can't –'

'Oh, yes, I can,' said Kranz. 'But you look too fit and well to be the victim of Nazi tyranny. We must change that. Now: what is your name?'

'Reissenburg. I demand to see –' He broke off as the Under officer struck him across the chest with a heavy whip. It seared across his flesh and he put up his arms, doubling over, clasping the pain to him, and stifling the scream that rose to his lips. He straightened, slowly.

'What is your name?'

'Max Reiss.'

'Where do you come from?'

'Reissdorf.'

'What did you do there?'

'Worked at the marine engine factory.'

'They will do worse than that to get the truth out of you, in England,' said Kranz, amiable. 'We must get you inured to such treatment.' He looked at the red weal across the muscled chest and smiled. 'Such a pity. You would be an excellent Nazi.'

They went out and Reissenburg sat on the bed, dismayed and angry that he had submitted so quickly.

The next day, they took the questions a little further. After the first three, Kranz went on: 'Why have you left Germany? You are not a Jew?'

'No.' Reissenburg hesitated. 'I am in trouble with the SS,' he proffered.

Kranz nodded. 'What sort of trouble?'

'I called Hitler a gutter-rat.' If they wanted the truth they could have it.

'Did you now,' said Kranz. 'Our informant did not tell us that. Are you sure it was nothing worse?' He looked into Reissenburg's mutinous face. 'Well – even that deserves correction.'

Reissenburg still had only his crumpled shorts. The whip seared three times across his naked back. Kranz smiled at the stifled gasps elicited.

'And what was the "gutter-rat" leading us to?'

'Defeat and destruction.' Another three lashes.

'Anything else?'

'I don't remember – Scapa Flow – another Versailles –'

'Quite enough to get you into trouble with the SS,' agreed Kranz. 'And how did you get away from them?'

'I don't know.'

'Three more to help him think, Meier,' said Kranz and strolled to the door.

When they had gone, Reissenburg dropped on to the bed, choking back tears. Oh, my Father, would you have given in so easily?

The next day, Kranz asked if he had thought how he was going to get away from the SS. He shook his head.

'I will tell you then,' the SS Colonel said. 'First, you will re-affirm your oath to the Fuhrer, Adolf Hitler.'

'I can't. I am dead.'

Kranz contemplated him. To an extent, that was true. The man who had sworn that oath was declared missing, presumed dead.

'Your death has not been confirmed,' he pointed out, patiently. 'You are missing.'

'Very well I re-affirm my oath to the Fuhrer, Adolf Hitler.'

'Next, you will swear to carry out to the limit of your ability those tasks assigned to you by our Agent who will contact you on arrival in England.'

'I swear.'

'It would not be in keeping with your aristocratic honour to break that oath,' sneered Kranz. 'You will be given appropriate papers when you leave. And the journey – there is one final, organized refugee transport leaving Bremerhaven next month. You will sail with it.' He looked at the semi-naked body. 'You still don't look as if you have suffered too much tyranny.'

That time, they beat him senseless.

4

The refugee ship had been chartered by American Jews but was calling at the Port of London before crossing the Atlantic to disembark those who had relatives in England or who could not afford the fare to New York.

Max Reiss, as his documents proclaimed him to be, had been given back his grey suit, somewhat crumpled with a striped cotton shirt and badly scuffed shoes. His own shirt rough dried and badly ironed and tie were with his other things in the overnight bag – including the change of underwear he so badly needed. But he was not given time to change nor to shave and was dispatched with a suitably-rough-looking 'relative' as guard to see him off at Bremerhaven. The car that took them from Hamburg, to which they had flown, stopped short of the docks and they joined the shuffling crowd making for the ship's berth. Reiss was well aware of the gun his escort held in his pocket and boarded the ship without any attempt to make a break for it. He did not, however, go through the farce of waving farewell to his 'grieving relation' who remained on the quayside until the gangway was removed and there was no chance of anyone 'jumping ship' except into the water.

At around fourteen to fifteen knots, Max Reiss reckoned the voyage to London would take some twenty-eight to thirty hours, so one night aboard. He did not bother to seek his berth but, having watched Bremerhaven fade into the distance, he went to bath and shave. As a refugee ship, as many passengers as possible had been packed into its cabins and saloons. He had been given a second-class passage and he found the wash-place mercifully empty. He pulled off his jacket and looked in his overnight bag to find his towel and shaving kit. An exclamation behind him made him swing round.

An elderly Jew in a long-coated black suit and a black hat had come in. For a long moment the fair young Aryan and the black-bearded Jew stared at each other.

'You are not one of us,' said the old man. 'But the SS have left their sign on your back. Do you escape from the Nazis?'

'Yes.' Max tried to look at his shoulders in the inadequate glass. The shirt, he realised, was stuck to him.

'The double zigzag of lightning,' said the old man. 'In blood and pus on your shirt. Have you another?' Max nodded. He could not remember ever having been addressed by a Jew before. The old man smiled.

'You must get in the bath with your shirt on,' he said. 'In that way you will soak it free. You cannot pull it off as it is. I will fetch some lotion to anoint you when you are ready.'

A month back Manfred Reissenburg's reaction would have been to tell the old Jew to get lost. Today, looking into the compassionate eyes, he knew a vast change had occurred in their relationship. He ducked his head.

'You are kind,' he said and went into one of the bath cubicles.

When he came out, the striped shirt rolled up in a towel almost as wet, Emmanuel Levi was waiting there, holding a bottle. When he saw the mutilation of the fair skin he cried out.

'Oh, my son! Why did they do this to you?'

Ten minutes later, bathed, shaved, eased and dressed, Max Reiss went up on deck. It was a fine June day and the sea was calm, flecked with dancing light from the sun. He sat down on a bench, alongside the centre structure by the accommodation ladder leading to the bridge. For a while he watched the sea and the sky and his shattered spirit cried out for his lost ship, his career, his home and family. Then he began to watch his fellow passengers. Jewish families stripped of their possessions, perhaps shopkeepers with their windows smashed and their goods looted or burnt. Kicked, spat upon, reviled, made sport of – yet going forth to a new and unknown life with resilience, even laughter. Very well, Max Reiss would meet his new life in the same way. He had known his course when he had re-affirmed his oath to Hitler; now he must work out how best to set about it. After a while, he went to seek out the old Rabbi.

So it was that when those refugees who were to disembark at the port of London were filing down the gangway, there was an unseemly disturbance. An old Jew had jostled a young Aryan who had turned on him and threatened him. The young man was soon pulled away by two sailors supervising the head of the gangway but he continued to fight until overpowered and the dockyard police were sent for. No-one noticed the exchange of looks between blue eyes and black as the old man turned to go down the gangway and the young was hauled to the bridge ladder and up to the Captain's day cabin.

The captain was displeased. He had enough to do, turning his ship round for the next leg of the journey, the eight or nine day passage to New York, without having a miscreant to deal with. However, the young man seemed quiet enough now, although holding himself rather stiffly as if his shoulders hurt him.

'Who are you?' the captain asked, resignedly. What the devil was this blond kraut doing in a Jew ship anyway? 'Why did you threaten the old man?'

'My name is Max Reiss,' said Max and his authoritative tone startled the Captain. 'I want to see the Police Inspector here.'

'You mean you deliberately created a disturbance in order to see the Inspector?'

'Yes. There is somebody meeting me – a German Agent. I do not want to be taken by him.'

'An Agent? A spy? But – you are a German national?'

'Yes. Please, Captain – I must see the Inspector – or Naval Intelligence.'

21

The Captain eyed him, assessing his genuineness. Then he turned to the Dockyard Police Sergeant.

'Sergeant, take this man to Inspector Radcliffe. Do not go through the Customs Shed – I take it you don't want to be seen by this Agent, Reiss? – but see if you can identify the man waiting.'

Inspector Radcliffe repeated this last instruction when the Sergeant had related the circumstances as he knew them and when he had gone, waved Max to a chair.

'Now, then, Mr. Rice,' he said. 'What is this all about? Why is a German Agent meeting you and why don't you want to meet him?'

'I am an officer of the Kriegsmarine and I have no intention of spying for Hitler.'

'And that was why you were sent over here as a refugee – or as a "German migrant" – no doubt with false papers.'

Max did not answer. He felt slightly sick. But the die was now cast and there was no drawing back. The Inspector waited a moment then picked up the telephone.

'Get me the Admiralty, please,' he said. 'Naval Counter Intelligence.'

The Sergeant returned as he finished his phone call.

'I found the man, sir,' he said. 'Had a chat, got his name and phone number and said we'd let him know if his "young relative" turned up.'

'Good. Commander Pallant is coming from Admiralty. Send him in directly he arrives.'

Alone with what he took to be a defector, the Inspector quietly assessed him and opened a conversation. The young German answered him politely enough but did not seem over-inclined to talk. Radcliffe made some notes to give to the Commander, starting with 'claims to be a naval officer.'

'Where have you come from?' he asked.

'From Berlin.'

'Your home?'

'No. SS headquarters.'

'SS?' Radcliffe was surprised. 'They have sent you here?'

'No – the Abwehr sent me. The SS were instructing me in British brutality.'

'They suggested we would get information from you by force?'

'Yes.'

Radcliffe noted the stiff shoulders and added to his list 'SS? beating.'

Commander Pallant, when he arrived some twenty minutes later, proved to be a tall, rangy man in civilian dress, dark-haired and with dark, piercing eyes. He fixed Max Reiss with a penetrating stare as the young man stood up. He noted the crumpled suit was of good quality and cut, that the scuffed shoes were of fine leather, that the strained face bore the indefinable stamp of good breeding. He nodded to Radcliffe.

'What is your name?'

'Max Reiss.'

'How old are you?'

'Twenty-three.'

'OK.' He took Reisse's documents and Radcliffe's notes. 'Thanks, Inspector. Is that the agent's name? Right. I'll take this lad with me. Is that all your kit?'

During the journey through the dockland areas, Pallant studied the German documents and Radcliffe's notes. He roused himself to point out the Tower.

'Not expecting to end there, are you?'

Max looked at it but did not reply. They went along the Victoria Embankment, into Whitehall Place and the rear of the Admiralty. Pallant's office looked on to a corner of the Horse Guards and his assistant, a Lieutenant Jeffries, awaited them. Pallant sat down at his desk, told Max to sit down and sent for coffee.

'Let's start again,' he said. 'What is your name?'

'Max Reiss.'

'Is that your real name or the one they have given you?' He tapped the passport.

'It is the name given to me.'

'So what is your name and rank?'

Max shook his head. 'I am dead. So I have no rank.'

Jeffries poured out coffee and distributed cups. Pallant sat back in his chair, stirring his coffee and staring at Max.

'You are dead,' he repeated. 'You are a young man. Do your parents know – whether you are alive or dead?'

'All my – kit – is at home. I am missing, presumed dead with just these clothes. If I do not carry out my assignments, my death will be confirmed.'

'And what are your assignments?'

'I don't know. I was to be told by my contact.' He swallowed the hot coffee, thirstily. Jeffries refilled his cup.

'You evaded him at the docks. Have you any other meeting place in the event of missing each other?'

'Yes. Waterloo Station at twelve noon tomorrow.'

'Are you prepared to make this contact – and inform us of your assignments?'

'Yes.' The word was curt, the white face rigid.

'It's not easy being a traitor, is it?' said the Commander, pleasantly. He saw the words cut home to the heart. But the heart was steadfast.

'I am a traitor,' acknowledged Max. 'I swore allegiance to Adolf Hitler. But not to my country which he betrays.'

'Your country,' repeated Pallant, softly. 'You are faithful to your country and want to rid it of the Nazis?'

'Yes. But we cannot do it alone. You do not understand the hold he has on us – the fear of the SS – the death camps.' He stopped abruptly.

Pallant nodded, slowly and picked up the telephone.

'Get me Colonel Sherriff at the Tower, please,' he said and smiled at Max. 'Not to worry. Ah, Colonel – I'm bringing you an inmate for a few nights – In your hospital wing, please. I want him checked over when he arrives. Yes, coming now. See you, shortly.' He put down the telephone. 'Just in case you're being tracked. You'll be safe, there.'

5

The Colonel, the Commander and the Doctor all sat in the Colonel's office and the subject of their discussion was the young German naval defector.

'He's basically a fit young man,' said the doctor. 'Suffered some ill-treatment over the last few weeks. Lack of food, some mental strain and, of course, the lashing. Scars suggest it was done over a couple of weeks, the most recent a few days ago when that obscene lightning logo was carved on. It'll heal all right but it will leave its outline.'

'The double lightning flash – or the double S,' said Sherriff. 'Of course, they will have marked him like that to mislead us. I gather the more fanatical Nazis are quite masochistic.'

'The normal SS tattoo is under the armpit, I believe,' said Pallant. 'But that wouldn't do to mislead us. They had to make out he was running from persecution. Anyway, we'll get him to Waterloo and take it from there.'

'But you think he might be back here for a bit?'

'Yes. I doubt if he'll stay with the Agent. 'I'll go and talk to him if it's OK?'

'Yes, certainly,' said the Colonel and the Commander and the Doctor went out.

Pallant was in uniform today and Max Reiss, who was standing looking out of the window of his small room, turned and snapped to attention. His overnight hold-all was packed and ready on the bed.

'All right, Max,' said Pallant. 'At ease.' He saw the faint distaste that his use of the name provoked. 'You will probably be coming back here, you know.'

'Yes, Commander. But I think, perhaps, I spent the night at the station.'

'Good thinking,' said Pallant.

'So, also, it would be better if I were there quite early.'

Pallant scratched his earlobe. Cocky little bugger, he thought.

'I agree,' he said, gravely. 'We will get you there by eleven. You will be under surveillance, of course and we will pick you up once your contact has gone. He may want you to go somewhere with him but I do not think it likely.'

'No, sir.' Max Reiss drew a slightly quivering breath and Pallant thought he was not quite so assured as he looked and sounded.

'Don't worry,' he said, with a smile. 'We'll look after you.'

'Yes. I am sorry. This is – strange to me.'

He showed no lack of assurance, Pallant, back in civvies, noted as the contact was made on the Waterloo Station concourse. Having established recognition he said curtly, 'Where were you yesterday? I expected you to meet me off the ship.'

Alec Barker, the contact, a rather weedy man nearing thirty, an adherent of Mosley and a fervent admirer of Hitler and his SA, was taken aback by this approach. He was supposed to be the one in charge, advising this newcomer what to do. He began to bluster.

'I was there. You did not come off with the Jews and the others.'

They walked out of earshot and Pallant sat down on a seat to wait. He could see Jeffries strolling along behind them, looking up at platform destinations. After some minutes, Max Reiss came back alone. At a little distance Jeffries followed. Pallant got up and Max paused by him as if to ask directions.

'Go out and get a taxi to Admiralty,' said Pallant. 'We'll be right behind.'

Jeffries joined Pallant.

'The contact caught a train on the Richmond line,' he said. 'He gave Reiss a note and what I imagine to be some English money. They didn't talk much – but our lad was definitely cock of the dung heap.'

'It's a bit clottish of them to give someone like Reiss a common little shit like that as a contact.' They were walking to the car.

'You think Reiss is a naval officer? The contact, I'm pretty sure, is a Black shirt called Barker. Lives near Twickenham.'

'He's only one of a network. Well – we'll see what he has to say.'

In Pallant's office, Reiss handed over a piece of paper on which was written Alec Barker and a telephone number, neither the same as given to the Dockyard Police Sergeant. He also had a wad of used banknotes which Pallant told him to keep.

'I don't suppose you'll use them to escape,' he said, with a grin.

'Escape! Where to?' asked Reiss, bitterly.

Pallant looked at his watch. 'Get some sandwiches and coffee sent up, will you, Jeff?' he said and settled back in his chair. 'Now, Max. What do they want?'

'Nothing at present. I am to apply for asylum, residency and a work permit and establish myself as a good citizen in preparation for the coming war.'

'As a marine engineer, you expect to be working near docks, perhaps naval bases?'

Reiss nodded, bleakly.

'When I get a job, I am to contact him on that number.'

'But suppose you are refused a work permit and interned as an undesirable alien?'

Reiss shrugged – and regretted it. He murmured the equivalent of 'So what?' in his own language and Pallant smiled.

'Or did you come to us to ensure that you were accepted? A double Agent, perhaps?'

The slightly supercilious blue gaze rested on Pallant's face.

'You have no reason to trust me, of course. I will have to be a double Agent, to carry this off. But you will know where I am, you will know what information I pass on.'

Pallant was silent, considering. He took the coffee and a sandwich from Jeffries.

'Tell me,' he said, suddenly. 'What did it mean to you when the SS said you were missing, believed dead and were to go to England?'

Reiss stared at him, recalling his desperation. For a brief moment, Pallant saw, his guard was broken, there was a long silence.

'I can't tell you,' Reiss said, at last. 'To lose home, family, career, identity, all at once, can you not think what it means?'

'Did they offer you any return?'

'Yes. If I – succeed – they will resurrect me as a hero of the Reich.'

'So you will be working for resurrection?'

'No.' The anguish was showing through. 'They can do that only if they win. And that will mean the death of Europe. How long will England survive if Hitler rules Europe? At present he says he admires you and your Empire, that if you let him take Europe, you can go on ruling your Empire. Can you believe that? Then, when he has you and your Empire, he will have half the world. But, if you withstand him…' A tiny smile twisted his lips, '…You can resurrect me.'

Pallant gazed at him for a long while, revolving what he had said in his mind.

'How,' he said, slowly, 'have you come to terms with your losses?'

'The Jews,' said Reiss. 'The Jews on the ship. Yes, a lot still had their families but we had stripped them of everything else: of their livelihood, life as they had known it, their homes and possessions. I was in no worse case – except for my family, who are safe.'

'You are satisfied that they are safe?'

'Yes. There is no quarrel with them.'

'What was the quarrel with you?'

'I insulted the Fuhrer.'

'In public!'

'I spoke to a British Naval officer in a café. We were talking. I think the waiter must have understood English and reported me.'

'A British Officer? You knew him?'

'I had seen him before. A Commander Hillman.'

Pallant glanced at Jeffries to check up on this, later. 'We'll get you back to the Tower,' he said.

Reiss looked at him and Pallant's dark, penetrating gaze watched the painful struggle between an arrogant spirit and the need to confess a weakness.

'Please – a little longer.'

'Have you more to tell us?'

Reiss shook his head. 'Just – the Tower – so long alone.'

Pallant was not an unsympathetic man. He could imagine a little of what Max Reiss was going through in the battle between his loyalties, his upbringing and his instinctive rejection of the Hitler regime and reaction to the SS brutality and the severance from his life and career and home. He could not imagine – nor, he thought, could anyone imagine – the depths of despair and agony such a situation must bring, not only to this young man but also to the Jews with whom he had identified himself, without experiencing it personally.

'How much money did Barker give you?' he asked.

'About a hundred pounds, to pay for lodging. He said I should go to the library reading-room to find work advertised.'

'Yes. Well, you've some money to spare to replenish your wardrobe. Some clothes suitable for an apprentice marine engineer, say. Jeffries, how do you fancy a shopping trip? You can deliver him at the Tower when you've done. I'll ask the Governor to give you some exercise in company by the river, Max. I don't think you'll find it like the SS.'

Jeffries returned a couple of hours later. 'I've left him with one of the Warders,' he said. 'Ex-Sergeant-Major, telling him all about the Beefeater uniform and the history of the Tower and how the ravens are brought from Devon.'

'Good. I've checked on Commander Hillman. He's based at Devonport at present. Ship's at sea and was on a courtesy call in Hamburg just before Christmas. I think we'll soon know the identity of our young cock sparrow.'

6

HMS *Billericay* had just returned to port and Commander Hillman, all duties accomplished for the present and the ship comfortably secured in her berth, was taking a few minutes' relaxation in his cabin when a messenger from the OOD on the gangway came to him.

'There's a Commander Pallant here, sir, asking to see you. From Admiralty.'

Henry, surprised, bestirred himself and preceded the messenger upsides. 'Commander Pallant?' he said. 'Hillman. Will you come below?'

'Thanks. I shan't keep you long.'

The wardrobe was relatively empty and Henry called for pre-lunch G&Ts and settled his visitor in a deep armchair.

'What can I do for you?'

'Can you think back to before Christmas, a café, probably in Hamburg and a conversation with a German naval officer who insulted Hitler?'

Henry regarded him speculatively.

'He called him a little gutter-rat leading them to defeat and destruction,' he said.

'Did he mean it or was he trying to impress you?'

'Oh, he meant it.'

'Who was he?'

Henry took a swig of gin. 'First – who are you and why do you want to know?'

'Naval Intelligence. I'll tell you the story when I know who he is.'

'Leutnant zur See Manfred von Reissenburg, elder son of the Admiral-Graf,' said Henry.

'Oh, my God!' said Pallant and emptied his glass.

'I take it his remarks have got him into trouble,' said Henry and signalled for refills. 'Where is he?'

'In the Tower – for safe keeping. Here's the story.'

When he had finished, Henry invited him to stay for lunch, then sat back to digest the bones of the tale.

'Are you going to use him?' he asked, at last.

'Oh, yes.'

'And if – when we are at war?'

'If I followed his thinking correctly, only our defeat of Hitler will save Germany and Europe. I think he will do his best to help us to that end.'

'Against his own people? His own service? He has a young brother – a naval cadet. He'll be torn apart.'

Pallant considered this. 'It's not as though he came here of his own accord. He was sent here – he was given no choice. To spy. The alternative, presumably, disgrace, imprisonment, a death camp?'

'And he paralleled his situation with that of the Jews?'

'Yes. I thought that was rather a good sign.'

The wardrobe mess was beginning to fill for lunch.

'Will you keep me informed so far as you can?' asked Henry. 'My father was acquainted with the Admiral at the end of the Great War and thought rather well of him. I was not entirely sure of the son when I saw him but I'd like to know what becomes of him.'

'I'll keep in touch,' said Pallant and they went into lunch.

A couple of weeks later, Pallant went to the Tower. He was taken to one of the enclosed, walled gardens where he found Max Reiss lying on the sunlit grass reading one of the books he had purchased on the shopping trip with Jeffries. The sound of the busy traffic on the Thames made a pleasant background.

'Don't get up,' said Pallant and sat down on the grass. 'I've got you a job. I had it in mind when I heard where Barker lived but I thought you'd better not find work too quickly. I've arranged for your work permit and alien's registration.'

'Where do I work?'

'A small boat-builders and marine engineers on the Thames – at Lock Road, Teddington.'

'Teddington?'

'It's the end of the tidal reach of the Thames – Tide-end-town – and quite near to Twickenham where Barker lives. About fifteen miles out of London.'

'I will be in touch with you.'

'Oh, yes. We shan't abandon you. Barker will probably be in favour of the post because the National Physical Laboratory is at Teddington. Admiralty experimental station.'

'Am I expected to break into that and send all the secrets to Barker?'

Pallant laughed. 'I don't think you'd get far. But he might expect that you would pick up talk in the town.'

Reiss smiled, reluctantly. 'I don't think I am very good at this. I visit the local inns?'

'Don't worry. Just settle into the job and become a good citizen. We shall let you know when we want you to pass on information.' Pallant got to this feet and the young German rose politely with him. 'I'll bring your documents and train ticket on Monday morning. So you've a couple more days to relax. Goodbye.'

Reiss ducked his head in the curt, sharp little bow but did not speak.

'I could almost feel sorry for him,' Pallant remarked to Jeffries when he got back to his office.

'Do we keep him to ourselves or go to the Circus?' asked Jeffries.

'Chief says keep him to ourselves,' said Pallant. 'We'll try him out for a year, say and then we might have a different way to use him.'

'Back in Europe? Do we let his family know he's safe?'

'No. Not yet, anyway.'

In a third-class compartment of a mid-morning train drawing out of Waterloo Station on Monday, Max Reiss also wondered about his family. He had with him a small suitcase, part of his recent purchases which it also contained and the overnight bag with which he had left home to go to Berlin with hopes of a new posting. He did not dwell on the horror that had followed his arrival in Berlin but he wondered how the news of his disappearance had been broken and how his family had received it. Not an auspicious start at the Naval Academy for Baldur.

He had a newspaper which he tried to read but it was full of the rumblings of war – as seen by the other side. But he could not look at it like that now. It was his side now – it had to be.

Clapham Junction, Wimbledon. You will cross the river after Kingston, Pallant had said and the second stop after that will be Teddington. Cross over the footbridge and turn left out of the station. Turn right into the High Street and keep straight on. When you come to the river, stop. You'll be in Brough Bros. yard. He suppressed a shiver and stared out of the window.

The instructions were simple enough to follow. He surrendered his ticket and turned left but stopped at the junction of the road from the station with the High Street to get the feel of the little town. The early July sun glared down on clean, open streets. To his left, the road rose to surmount the railway track. Opposite, beyond a small triangle of trees and lying back from a broad expanse of pavement was the local cinema. Over the bridge came a red trolley bus which pulled up a little further down the High Street. Again over the bridge and going off to the left came a red motor bus numbered 65. For a small place, Reiss felt it was well-served with public transport. He walked on along the High Street. Not very exotic but perhaps it was the glaring sun that made him remember Georgetown and Commander Hillman.

Two churches made him pause: a lowly stone one with ancient gravestones in the churchyard to his left and a tall, modern one to his right, cathedral-like with a bright green copper roof. But the road went straight on between them and so did he. A junction with traffic lights faced him but, straight on, lay a short stretch, signed Lock Road, bordered by cottages and, at the end, a broad ramp, sloping down to the river, on which were pulled up several rowing skiffs and a small cabin cruiser. To the left a big shed with 'Brough Bros., Boat Builders. Marine Engineers' emblazoned above the double doors.

Reiss walked across to it and pushed open the small door inset into one of the big ones. Inside, one set of stocks was occupied by a cabin cruiser, presumably under repair. Another held a smaller boat under construction. The two men working on this glanced up at him but did not stop their work. From the deck of the cruiser, another man, of between forty to fifty years, looked down at him.

'Mr. Brough?' he said and his voice, trained to carry at sea, sounded authoritative and commanding in the confines of the shed. The two boat builders exchanged glances.

'That's me, son,' said the man on the cabin cruiser. 'Come up here and we'll have a chat.'

Max Reiss put down his bags and climbed the ladder to the boat's deck. Brough held out a hand and studied him frankly.

Ted Brough had joined the Merchant navy at fourteen and been commissioned as an Engineer Officer RNR on the outbreak of the Great War. He had come through virtually undamaged and in 1920 had joined his father and uncle – the Brough Bros. of the sign – in the family business. Since their retirement he was the sole Brough but was hoping to change that to Brough & Son in a few years' time. His new employee interested him because Commander Pallant had given him the two stories. For public consumption Reiss had got into trouble with the SS and fled to England for asylum as a refugee. For his own private knowledge he had been given the bare bones of the truth.

'You will be what the Circus call his case officer,' said Pallant. 'But he does not know that you've anything to do with

35

Naval Intelligence. Keep an eye on him, let me know his movements and we'll see if they tally with what he tells me.'

Brough's first impression was quite favourable: a slim, fit-looking young man who met his gaze levelly if a shade disdainfully. Knowing so much of his history Brough could accept that, at present, anyway. If it persisted, he had learned in the RNR how to deal with it. He led the way into the cabin and sat down.

'All right, Reiss,' he said. 'Sit down. Now, what do you know about this work?'

'About boat-building, very little. I was in a marine engineering works where we made engines – so two-stroke, four-stroke, direct or indirect drive, geared, diesel electric – but I do not know much of the theory, of the power needed for the size of ship, so on.'

'Well, that's frank enough. I expect you'll soon get to know about the engines we deal with. Mostly repair work, of course. Come along. We'll have a bit of dinner and I'll show you around afterwards.' He went out on deck. 'Joe! I'm off to my dinner.'

The older of the boat-builders raised a hand.

7

Brough had decided to lodge his German migrant in his home. He had a large, Victorian house with lawns running down to the river, reached from the back of his shed by a path into his garden or, at the front, from the road running to Twickenham. He had married his wife, Rosemary, whom he called Rosie, soon after joining the business and their children were Paul, aged fifteen who was to become the '& Son' and Deanna, aged twelve. Paul cycled into Kingston Grammar School each day and his sister to the Convent School at Hampton Wick. They would soon be starting their summer holidays.

Max Reiss was a bit disconcerted at this place of lodging but Rosie Brough showed him to a decent-sized bedroom at the back of the house, pointed out the bathroom and what she called 'the needful' and told him to come down to dinner when he had washed because Deanna had to get back for afternoon school.

Dinner proved to be cottage pie with vegetables and apple tart and custard and Ted Brough offered his employee a glass of beer which he refused. So Brough quaffed his own and kept a sharp eye open for signs of disdain. But Max Reiss ate what he was given and treated both Rosie and Deanna with courtesy. The child in her school frock and navy-blue blazer watched him, covertly.

The skiffs on the ramp, Reiss discovered during his tour that afternoon, were a summer sideline, and hired out by the hour to anyone fancying a row on the river. The suspension bridge to the right of the ramp was a favoured idling spot where people stood and watched the placid activity around. At the foot of the slope leading on to the bridge an ice-cream man took up

37

position with his box tricycle and did a good trade in ice-cream blocks, wafers and 'Sno-fruits' which were fruit-flavoured water ices in triangular cardboard wrappers.

Reiss accepted without a blink Brough's remark that anyone near when a skiff was wanted slid it down to the water and embarked the rowers, provided them with oars, slotted in the rudder and took their two shillings for an hour on the Thames. He wondered a bit at Pallant's choice of employment for him but decided he had to prove himself a good citizen before he got to a place where he could be of any use – to either side. He was then taken back into the big shed where the cabin cruiser's engine had been lifted out and put on a bench, given some overalls and told to strip it down.

It was some years since he had been in the Reissbaden works but his grounding had been thorough. His native efficiency had also made him buy a book on marine engines which he had studied while in the Tower. So he was not unduly perturbed as he took off his jacket, pulled on the overalls and set to work. Brough watched him with growing appreciation.

He learned, sometime later, that 'Brough Bros.' had another large shed at the top of Ferry Road; devoted to their marine engineering and that they had an Admiralty contract. Most of the engineering staff worked up there unless Brough needed someone down at Lock Road for repair work. Otherwise Joe and the other boat-builder, Bob, were the main ones down there. And when the school holidays started, young Paul Brough came in and dealt with most of the skiff hire.

They seemed to accept him reasonably well. Paul eyed him a bit askance at times. Bob sometimes threw the odd jibe at him. Brough and the older man, Joe, just took him as he was, noting that he was prepared to work hard and not to question the jobs he was given.

But it was neither the work nor the life to satisfy him, trained to take responsibility for a ship of war and her complement of men. It tried his patience. Neither Barker nor Pallant had got in touch with him. He took to walking and exploring the district and found a Carnegie library, down Waldegrave Road, beyond the cinema. He did not join it as a borrower but used the reading and reference rooms occasionally on a Saturday afternoon. On Sundays he crossed the river and went over Ham Fields to Richmond Park or through the town, past the National Physical Laboratory to Bushy Park where the stately trees of the Chestnut Avenue had long shed their candles and were setting their prickly fruit.

August came in. Young men and women were applying to join the forces. Paul was bemoaning the fact that he had over two years to wait before he could apply. Rosie Brough was hoping that his father's work would exempt him from the armed forces and kept silent.

'They'll be taking you off to an internment camp soon, Max,' jeered Bob. 'Like they did with Jerries last time.'

They were taking the mid-morning break out in the hot, heavy sunshine by the skiff shed. Brough and Joe watching Paul skim flat pebbles on the water. Bob continued his grumbles and uttered an obscene insult. For a moment it seemed the two would come to blows but Max restrained himself with an effort. Not before Joe had caught Bob's arm and Ted Brough had grabbed Max by the shirt collar. He wrenched himself free but the shirt, loose, came half off and Brough let go as if it were a hot potato. Max shrugged it on to his shoulders again and turned, his head lifted arrogantly and his eyes daring Brough to speak. He walked into the big shed.

'What the bloody hell was all that about?' demanded Bob.

Brough looked at Joe. 'The scars,' he said. 'Of Nazi beatings.'

'So that's why he left Germany,' said Joe.

When he went back into the shed, Brough said quietly to Max, 'I'm sorry, lad. We didn't know.'

Their attitude was subtly changed and Reiss had to admit, grimly, that the SS were, perhaps, right in giving visible proof of his need to defect.

On Sunday, 3rd September, he was standing on the end of the lock, watching a pleasure steamer and a cabin cruiser enter the biggest one on the Surrey side when the air-raid alarm was sounded, soon after eleven o'clock. One of the lock-keepers who had come to the end to shut the big lock gates, looked at him and observed 'Quick off the mark! We only just declared war!' He paused, watching the water begin to rise to bring the boats up to the level of the non-tidal upper reach. Like all the keepers he was a retired naval man, in his case a Chief Petty Officer. 'To old for recall now,' he sighed. 'But I went through the last lot.' He found his listener attentive and added 'Was in HMS *Broke* when we rammed the Jerry. We lowered a boat to pick up survivors.' He chuckled. 'When they grabbed the gunwale we just rapped their knuckles with an oar. They soon let go.' He touched a finger to his cap and walked off.

Reiss, outwardly unmoved for the story was not unknown, was yet sick at heart. So it had come. Poland invaded despite the Anglo-Polish Pact and Britain driven into war. Baldur, a seventeen-year-old cadet. To what ship would he be posted? Reiss crossed over the gates to the towpath and began to walk along it, towards Kingston. Across the river, by the Weir, were the gardens and lawn of the Anchor Inn and of big, private houses, many of them with craft of varying sizes tied up to their landing stages. The pleasure steamer, released from the lock, sailed majestically past, crowded with trippers on the way to Hampton Court Palace. The little cabin cruiser putted in its wake and a shirt-sleeved young man at its wheel waved to the solitary watcher on the bank. Reiss raised a hand in response and then wiped it across his face to remove the tears that had escaped. That young man was probably awaiting his call-up, no doubt, as a weekend sailor, into the Naval Volunteer Reserve. And he, himself, where might he have been but for his disastrous talk with Hillman and the visit to Berlin? At sea, in a commerce raider? Standing by, to commission *Bismarck* on her completion? He sat down on the coarse grass of the sloping river bank, staring across the grey water, because the tears would not stop rolling down his cheeks.

He got back to Brough's house late afternoon and went up to his room. A few minutes later a knock on the door heralded Ted Brough.

'Well – it's started, Max,' he said. 'Took a good walk, did you, lad? It's upsetting but we've been expecting it long enough. I just hope it will be over before my Paul's old enough. Mother thinks he'll be reserved – for the business – but it won't be while I'm still active, though. Anyway, I didn't come up to gossip but to tell you the police want you to report, in person, once a week. Start tomorrow, nine o'clock.'

'Yes; thank you. That is all right with you?'

'If the police want it, that's it.'

So, at nine o'clock that Monday morning, Max Reiss reported with his papers at the small police station. He was surprised to be taken into the Inspector's office. That worthy inspected the documents he presented, gave them back and sat back to regard him.

'I've got a phone number for you,' he said. 'A Commander Pallant. You'd best call him from here.' He stood up, held out a slip of paper and left the office.

Pallant was concise. 'Call me from the police station if you're contacted. From nowhere else unless it's an emergency. If I want you, the police will let you know.'

After that, all was quiet again. The 'phony' war was in progress with no enthusiasm shown for its pursuit. Hitler completed his takeover of Poland and atrocity tales abounded. Bob, who had held off since the incident on the hot August day, began to make snide remarks again.

On the quiet stretch of river, below the suspension bridge, alongside the island between the Weir and the locks, Brough had a line of buoys to which sundry craft were secured. He had his regulars and the trot was filling up as the small boats began to come back and be laid up for the winter. The owner of one of them, a smart-looking little thirty-foot cabin cruiser with a roomy well-deck was General Carpenter.

8

General Ian Carpenter was probably nearer seventy than sixty, a long, stringy dried-up man with a face permanently tanned by the climates of India, Palestine and other areas of the Middle and Far East. He had a small house in the town but had lost his wife a few years back and now spent most of his days with his boat, cruising in the summer and just 'messing about' in the winter. He reported a spot of engine trouble when he tied up and Max Reiss was sent out to investigate. It was a minor fault and Max did not take long to correct it.

It was a mild, sunny October afternoon and the General invited him to take a seat on the stern-bench of the cockpit and have a cup of tea. He endeavoured to refuse but the general was an autocratic man and lonely.

'Sit down,' he said, testily. 'You're not English, are you?'

'No. I am German,' said Max, flatly.

The General paused in the doorway of the cabin, teapot in hand.

'What the devil are you doing here?' he said.

'I left Germany three months ago. I was in trouble with the SS.'

'The Gestapo?'

'No. Not the Geheimstaatspolizei. The Schutzstaffel.'

Carpenter grunted and brought out two mugs of tea.

'All one to me,' he said. 'What for?'

'Insulting Hitler.'

'Doesn't sound a very desperate crime to me,' said the General. 'What about the *Royal Oak* business, eh? And *Courageous*, only two weeks after war was declared.'

43

The sinking of HMS *Courageous* on September 17th had not seemed to arouse the country out of its apathetic approach to the war. Now U47's penetration of Scapa Flow and the torpedoing of HMS *Royal Oak* at anchor there had aroused more anger at the lack of defences and netting of the approach than at the appalling losses. Max wanted to say he knew Gunter Prien, admired his courage in making such a lone strike but he could not admit his naval connections nor commend an enemy commander.

'Tragedies of war,' he said.

'And you will be safely out of it?' said the General.

Max looked down into his mug. 'Yes,' he uttered. 'I will be safely out of it.'

'A young fellow like you,' said Carpenter. 'You want to be in it?'

Max lifted his head. 'I did not want to fight for Hitler,' he said. 'But yes, I want to be in it.'

'H'm.' The General put their mugs down on the bench seat. 'Be patient. Prove yourself. You may have a chance. I'll take you back to Brough's.'

They got into '*Mignonette*'s small tender and rowed across the short distance to the ramp.

Just after the middle of December the news reports were full of the raider named variously *Deutschland* or *Admiral Scheer* and eventually recognized as *Graf Spee* when she was accosted by the three British ships, *Exeter*, *Ajax* and *Achilles*. The ensuing battle, the suspense of her time in Monte Video, the scuttling and her Captain's suicide tore Max Reiss to pieces. He continued to work as efficiently but withdrew into himself and even Bob's jibes did not reach him. The police told him to telephone Pallant, who ordered him up to London, prepared to stay for a week.

He arrived at Pallant's office mid-morning on Christmas Eve and remembered that only a year ago he had arrived home and Baldur was sitting by the Christmas tree.

Pallant's dark eyes viewed him searchingly as he came in controlled, stiff-necked, stubborn and suffering.

'You are wishing you were back with your ship,' he said, abruptly.

'Of course. But what would await me if I went back now?'

'No – there's no going back.'

'I have not heard from Barker.'

'Nor will you. He was a Fascist and has been imprisoned with a lot of other Blackshirts.'

'So – what is my purpose? Should I get a gun and follow Langsdorff?'

'Did you know him?'

'I have served under him. I knew many in *Graf Spee*.'

'Yes,' said Pallant, dryly. 'I knew many in *Royal Oak*.'

Reiss acknowledged this, bleakly. 'Can you find out where my brother is?' he asked.

'I will try to get news for you. In the meantime I'm putting you back in the Tower for a week.'

Tiredly aloof blue eyes regarded him speculatively while Reiss digested this. 'I am glad. But why?'

Pallant smiled, his dark face lightening and softening.

'I don't think a family Christmas would be good for you or for the Broughs,' he said, gently. 'It will be different in the Tower.'

Reiss accepted this with a wry smile.

'Then I go back to Teddington? Is there nothing more active that I can do?'

'Not just at present. Hold out for another six months, will you? Then we will see.'

On his return, Reiss went up to the engine assembly shed. Apart from maintenance and overhaul of the boats laying up for the winter, Brough's main work was now under his Admiralty contracts. Reiss worked on engines destined for ships' lifeboats and launches and sometimes was sent to the trot to help the owners of small craft, including General Carpenter.

As spring approached, it was clear that the war in France was not going well for Britain. The loss of aircraft by bombing of the poorly-defended French airfields forced the decision to fly the surviving planes home. The question was mounting as to how the Expeditionary Force was to get back.

On a fine day in late May Reiss walked through Bushy Park to the Diana Fountain. The candles on the trees were beginning to bloom ready for Chestnut Sunday, traditionally the first Sunday in June. Some deer amongst the trees watched his passage and, finding nothing to alarm them, continued to graze. He was on his way back, between the churches, when General Carpenter caught up with him. The old man had an ancient carpet bag in his hand.

'I'm going to try out the boat this afternoon,' he said, abruptly. 'Come with me to check the engine. Bring a change of clothes in case we get stuck. Brough has OK'd it.'

Nothing loath, Max joined the *Mignonette* that afternoon. He had checked with Brough who had simply nodded and the thought of even a river trip was pleasing. Carpenter seemed a bit preoccupied and he had stocked his larder with tinned food and with drink. The engine started sweetly, Carpenter broke out the Red Ensign at the stern and they set off down river. Most of the other boats on the trot seemed to be preparing for pre-summer warm-ups and, from the lock above them, came the ocean-going steam yacht usually moored at the landing stage of one of the big houses above the Weir.

As they passed under Richmond Bridge, more small craft were joining them and Reiss began to see the amazing plan.

'You are going to rescue your troops from France,' he said to the General. 'And you chose me to help you?'

The General rubbed his chin. 'I asked Brough for someone. He told me to take you. It's a chance to prove yourself, Max.'

My God, thought Max, what a chance! Fascinated, he watched the converging craft, all manned by amateur sailors, some steered by girls in jerseys and slacks – what a nation of amateurs the British were – and how good at it they were. It was crazy, it was magnificent, it was inspiring – and only the British could have thought of such a solution and known that the call would be answered without question.

The following morning saw them creep out of the estuary to Sheerness. There they were gathered and sorted and re-fuelled. Where necessary, a naval officer took over but most owners clung tenaciously to their command. The General and his young engineer were accepted without question, given charts and sent on to Dover. As they rounded North Foreland, the General handed over the wheel and watched the obvious competence of his companion with grim understanding. He went below and came up with steaming cups of coffee.

'You're a sailor, aren't you Max,' he said. 'Navy or merchant marine?'

'Navy,' said Max Reiss. What did it matter? How many of them would come out of this alive?

'You insulted Hitler. Were you cashiered?'

'No. I was sent over here to spy.'

'So – you are a naval officer, with no uniform and false documents? You realize you could be shot?'

Max gave a short laugh. 'I should think it very likely,' he said. 'But not as a spy. I gave myself up to your counter-intelligence when I arrived.'

'Ah-h!' said the General, relieved. 'You are with us?'

'To defeat Hitler, yes. But I am German. It is my country.'

'But you are prepared to help rescue our troops?'

'As I would pick up survivors from a ship I had sunk.'

'But these will be escaping to freedom, not to captivity.'

'General – are you trying to make me put about?'

'No. I'm testing your strength of purpose. Believe me, Max, it will be tried sorely over the next days.'

At Dover they were re-fuelled again, entered on the inspecting officer's clipboard as '*Mignonette*, owner/skipper General Ian Carpenter; engineer Max Rice,' and their length and possible 'passenger' capacity noted. At first light they set off on the 39-mile trip to Dunkirk.

They met some of the 'little ships' coming back, grossly overloaded, their packed cargo woefully seasick with the motion. An old paddle steamer, *Medway Queen*, wallowed past them. A destroyer, her decks alive, strode commandingly through the straggling flotillas.

Nothing prepared them for the sight of the Dunkirk beaches. There were fires inland and what at first appeared to be long black breakwaters stretching out into the sea and proved, on closer sight, to be patient lines of soldiers, the leading files up to their thighs in water. A couple of destroyers were anchored offshore, their boats plying to and fro, picking up a load of men and ferrying them back, then setting off for the shore again.

'We do that?' suggested Reiss. 'There is no point in going back to Dover with each load.'

The General nodded, staring in appalled silence at the beach. As they passed the destroyers, the guns opened up as a wave of bombers swept out and along the seashore. Bombs fell and suddenly the tail end of one line of men disappeared in an eruption of sand, water and bodies. Behind came fighters, peppering the beaches with machine gun fire. The stoical lines in the sea stood firm and raised a cheer as the destroyers' guns brought down a fighter which crashed into the sea with a blaze of flame.

Carpenter, grim-faced, looked at his helmsman but Max was steadily bringing the craft up to the line of men and he had to turn his attention to them and help to haul them into the cockpit and cram them into the cabin or forward on to the deck.

All through the noise and confusion of the day, Mignonette loaded her soaking passengers and decanted them on to the destroyers. As one filled up, another slim, grey shape, usually with anti-aircraft guns blazing, moved up to take her place. Hardly knowing what he was doing, dragging bodies on board, the General yet had time to acknowledge Max's tireless expertise in coming alongside to disembark, then backing off and returning to the endless line of waiting men.

'General,' he called at last. 'We'll go back with this load in company with the destroyer. We shall need to refuel.'

Speechless, Carpenter nodded. The destroyer had been damaged in a bomb attack and, overloaded as they both were; they managed to creep back to Dover.

9

While hoping to rescue some 25,000 troops from Dunkirk, the 'little ships' eventually clawed back 350,000 and there began the defeat of Hitler. The old *Medway Queen* chugged back and forth and carried 7,000 to safety. How many little *Mignonette* hauled off, her exhausted crew did not know. They snatched some sleep on the dishevelled bunks, between late supper and early breakfast and set off again, with full fuel tanks, at first light. It was the end of May. Reiss was concerned about the old General and tried to get him to hand over to naval personnel. But the old man declared his toughness and they sailed again. If anything, the bombing and the machine-gunning attacks were intensified. The noise, the explosions, the flames, screams and shouts merged into one dreadful cacophony in which the task of rescue went on unceasingly. A company of Guards, marching down in perfect order as if on Horse Guards Parade, lifted morale considerably and the embarkation went on with renewed heart.

Around midday, *Mignonette* was about to pull away from the destroyer when a stick of bombs fell and the ship was straddled. There were screams from the stricken soldiers crammed on deck. *Mignonette* shuddered and, quietly, her bow disappeared. Reiss grabbed the General and pushed him to the ladder still suspended over the destroyer's side and willing hands pulled the old man on to the shambles of the deck. Max Reiss followed and glanced back to see the remains of *Mignonette* sink below the surface.

A sailor was fighting his way to the bridge ladder and perhaps seeing the General's air of authority said, 'I think the bridge copped it, sir.'

Carpenter and Reiss followed him up the ladder and found a scene of carnage on the open bridge. There was no-one alive.

'Is the First Lieutenant aft?' demanded Reiss.

The sailor looked surprised at his accent but recognized the air of command.

'Yes sir, but he's injured, bad, sir, he wouldn't get through.'

'Anyone on the wheel?'

'Yes, sir. The Quartermaster.'

Reiss looked forward. The anchor party marooned there on the forecastle by the press of soldiers was gazing anxiously towards the bridge.

'I think we go, General,' he said and signalled to the anchor party. 'Pass my orders,' he told the sailor and eased the ship slowly up to the anchor so it could be raised; with engines still slow ahead: 'Starboard ten.'

'Starboard ten, sir. Ten of starboard on, sir.'

The ship came round gently. With the overloaded decks it would not do to keel over.

'Ask the Chief how things are in the Engine room. What revs. can she give?'

The sailor bent o the voice-pipe.

'OK below, sir. Revs for twenty-five knots.'

'Steer two-seven-o.'

'Two-seven-o, sir.'

'Half ahead, both.'

The damaged destroyer set off on her westerly course, her surviving crew hampered in any repair efforts by the seething humanity she carried, so not going at her fullest possible speed. After a little, as she seemed to be handling quite well, Reiss felt confident enough to increase speed which made things easier. He was aware of the old General's encouraging presence and the sailor was accepting his command. He noted that the man had crossed flags on his arm, signifying signalman. The ship, he had seen on the bell, was HMS *Ditchling*.

Dover was suffering an air-raid as they approached and *Ditchling*'s guns opened up as the planes swept overhead. Who

51

was manning them, Reiss did not enquire nor whether the Gunnery Officer still lived.

A near-miss on the starboard side just abaft No. 2 gun flattened all three on the bridge. Reiss got up with a gash from a splinter along his upper arm, the sailor rose dazed but uninjured and bent to help the General to his feet, bleeding from a scratch on his forehead, all of them smeared with blood from the bodies.

'Signal for permission to come alongside. Report many dead and wounded,' Reiss told the signalman and the man took up a signalling lamp. Having learned which voice-pipe was which, he ordered, 'Slow ahead, both,' to the engine room.

'Slow ahead both, who the bloody hell are you?' was the response.

They were directed to a berth at a jetty where ambulances were already lining up and manoeuvred gently alongside. Brows were positioned fore and aft and disembarkation was hastened. Reiss 'finished with engines.'

The General and his 'engineer' went quietly down the bridge ladder and joined the exodus.

'I'm not sure of the penalty for hi-jacking a destroyer,' remarked Carpenter.

A Red Cross worker collared them as they came on to the quayside, classified them as 'walking wounded' and hurried them into a canvas covered ambulance. Taking the line of least resistance they went, thereby evading any recall from a highly indignant Lieutenant (E) who came to find out who was giving orders and stopped, silenced by the carnage on the bridge, now devoid of life. The officer in charge of the 'cleaning up' party, arriving at about the same time, looked around and said, 'Who the hell brought you home?'

That question was, later, being posed in an office in the depths of VA Dover's headquarters. The Base Captain, conferring with Admiral Ramsay remarked on it.

'*Ditchling* came in, filled to the brim with troops,' he said. 'And with every officer on the bridge, dead. The First

Lieutenant was aft and badly hurt, unable to get along the decks. The Engineer Officer knew nothing of the situation until the signalman on the bridge started passing orders and said the Captain and the Pilot were dead. He didn't say who he was taking the orders from but whoever it was brought her in faultlessly. When the Chief got up top there was no-one there.'

'Find that signalman,' said Ramsay, tersely. 'I don't believe in ghost crews.'

The signalman was brought in by a lieutenant-commander RNVR who had the typed list of small ships, some time later.

'A young man, sir,' he reported. 'Fair hair, came on board with an old gentleman he called "General" after their boat sank alongside us.'

'They were feeding *Ditchling* with troops from the beach. She was bombed and the boat was sunk. From the list it would seem likely to have been *Mignonette*.' The lieutenant commander checked his notes. 'Owned and skippered by General Carpenter and crewed by Max Rice. Came down to Sheerness from Teddington two or three days ago.'

'What made you take orders from him?' asked the Base Captain of the signalman.

'I dunno, sir. He seemed like he was naval. But he had an accent – I though he was Dutch or Norwegian, helping the General out.'

'Where did he and the General go?'

'I didn't see, sir. They both got it when we were bombed just outside Dover. The old man was a bit shaky.' He gulped. 'We all went down – on the bodies – and bits. The Dutchie just told me to signal for permission to enter harbour and go alongside to land dead and wounded. And the troops, of course.'

'I expect they've gone to a casualty centre, sir,' said the lieutenant-commander.

'See if you can trace them, Mathers, will you?' said the Base Captain. 'All right, Bunts, thank you. *Ditchling* will be in for repairs. You'd best report back to barracks.'

'Aye, aye, sir.'

In the meantime, Reiss and the General had been taken to a casualty department in a small hospital on the outskirts with some of the walking wounded from the ship, mostly soldiers from the Dunkirk beaches. As they were not in uniform they were mistaken for victims of the air-raid and sat waiting for attention until the old General began to suffer reaction.

'Those beaches,' he said. 'Oh, God, those poor boys. How many did we leave? We ought to go back for more, Max – come on...' He began to get agitated and Max caught a passing doctor who tried to brush him off.

'This man has come from Dunkirk,' said Max. 'Please attend to him.' His crisp, accented tones stopped the doctor.

'They've all come from Dunkirk,' he said and looked at the General. 'You mean...?'

'He has been rescuing troops. His boat was bombed.'

The General, to Reiss's relief, was guided away. He sat down again. The dressing on his arm was becoming saturated and he felt vaguely light-headed. It seemed a long time since breakfast and the lights in the cream-painted corridor were bright. Most of the soldiers had been attended to now and the staff nurse, walking briskly, paused to look at him.

'Come along,' she said. 'I'll clean that up for you. Air-raid?'

He nodded. It was not worth the bother of explaining. She took him into a treatment room and cut away the sleeves of his jersey and shirt and laid bare the gash.

'How did you get this?' she asked. 'It will need stitching. I'll find the doctor.' She didn't wait for the answer he had not attempted to give and left the room. When she came back it was with the doctor who had taken the General away. He looked at the wound and told her to prepare a local anaesthetic.

'Weren't you with the old man, the General?' he said.

'Yes.'

'Can you give me his name and address? If you're Max Rice, he's asking for you. I'll take you along when we've patched you up.'

Max gave the General's address as care of Brough Brothers. There was no point in naming an empty house. His numbed arm was stitched, bandaged and supported in a sling and the doctor took him to a crowded ward. The General was lying in a screened bed and looking very grey and frail.

He opened weary eyes. 'Did we get them all away, Max?' he whispered. 'Did we get them all off?'

'Yes, General, we brought them home.'

'Good. That's good, Max. I've done my bit, now. I've no more to give.'

It was here that Lieutenant Commander Mathers RNVR, having ascertained by telephone that this hospital had admitted a General Carpenter and treated his crewman, Max Rice, finally caught up with them. But Max Reiss refused to leave and remained by the bed, his hand clasped tightly until the worn-out old General at last let go and quietly followed his beloved boat to his everlasting rest.

Reiss, himself almost sleepwalking, came out of the ward and found Mathers, patiently waiting. He pulled himself together.

'I am sorry, Commander,' he said. 'I could not leave him to die alone.'

'I understand,' said Mathers. 'You came with him from Teddington?'

They went out to Mathers' car, into the darkening evening. When they got to base, the Captain was taking time out to snatch some dinner. Mathers asked if Rice had eaten. Not since breakfast at three-thirty that morning, thought Max, with the old General, tired but then alive.

'No,' he said.

A NAAFI canteen, catering non-stop for the crews from the small ships and from the naval craft, grabbing some quick food before setting off again, provided them with eggs, sausages and chips and big cups of coffee. There was no distinction between who ate there. They were all intent on the job in hand.

10

Captain Brett, his secretary and a Special Branch Commander were all in his office when Mathers and Reiss were sent for.

'Sit down, Mr. Rice,' said Brett, shaking hands. 'I understand General Carpenter died. I am sorry. You were a friend of his?'

'He kept his boat at the Brough Brothers yard where I am employed,' said Max Reiss. 'He asked me to come on – this trip – with him.'

'How long have you been employed there?'

'Nearly one year.'

'So you came over here before the war. From where, Mr. Rice?'

'From Germany.'

'You are a German national?'

'Yes.'

'Not a Nazi, then?'

'No.'

They contemplated him. The Commander took up the questions which, with the answers, the Secretary was writing down.

'The signalman in HMS *Ditchling* says you took command "in a naval manner" when everyone was killed on the bridge. How did you come to do that?'

Max Reiss paused. His weariness made him look detached and disdainful. He thought that Pallant would by now have got hold of Commander Hillman and would know who he was.

'I have served in destroyers,' he said. 'I am Leutnant zur See Reissenburg.'

'Bloody hell,' muttered the Commander, looking at him in blank astonishment.

Captain Brett leaned forward, his eyes bright with interest.

'You are a German naval officer?' he said.

'Yes, but a dead one,' thought Manfred von Reissenburg.

'Yes, sir,' he said.

'You realize,' Brett said, smiling, 'You could be taken to the Tower of London, tried and shot?'

Reissenburg achieved a return smile.

'I have a room in the Tower,' he said. 'Please contact Commander Pallant at Admiralty. He knows of me.'

Brett looked at the Commander, who nodded.

'Pallant's Counter Intelligence,' he said.

'Check it out, Mathers,' said Brett and glanced at his watch. 'If they're still awake.' Mathers left the room. 'And now,' continued Brett 'you have suffered an injury bringing our troops back from France. How do you reconcile that?'

'I see no hope for Germany until Hitler is destroyed. Perhaps he will be assassinated. Then the generals will take over and seek peace with you.'

'Ah! So you're not alone in your anti-Nazi movement?'

'No.' Reissenburg struggled to smother a yawn and Brett laughed.

'James,' he said to his secretary. 'Lend Leutnant Reissenburg the camp bed in your office and we'll go on with this, later.'

The Secretary returned with Mathers.

'He went out like a light,' he reported.

'Commander Pallant was very interested to hear of Max Reiss' adventures,' said Mathers. 'He confirms his rank, says he was overheard denigrating Hitler, beaten up by the SS and sent over here in a refugee ship. He gave himself up on arrival and was sent to one of our people in Teddington as a marine engineer. Elder son of Admiral Count Reissenburg. His brother is a naval cadet.'

'What does Pallant want us to do with him?'

'Send him up there when we've finished with him. He says he is trustworthy and can travel without escort.'

'Well, by God,' said Captain Brett. 'Here's a turn up for the books. A nice little traitor-cum-hero on our hands. Both he and the General would be in line for an award, of course!'

The four of them considered the implications of this. Then Brett sent for coffee and they turned their attentions to the progress of the evacuation.

When the Captain's Secretary woke him in the morning, Reissenburg was stiff from pulling soldiers from the sea and pushing them up the ladders to the destroyer's decks. He had taken off the sling before stretching out on the camp bed and blood and pus were seeping through the bandage. James took him along to the sickbay and left him there.

'They'll bring him back here when they've cleaned him up and fed him,' he said.

'That's fine,' said Brett, absently. His mind was on *Ditchling* and her appalling casualty list. The First Lieutenant had been taken off alive but unconscious, he and the engineer the only officers surviving. Two others had been killed, together with a number of the rescued soldiers they were helping to pull aboard, by the bomb that had sunk *Mignonette*. The Pilot, the OOW and the Captain had perished on the bridge with the Chief Yeoman of Signals and a couple of lookouts. The Gunnery and Torpedo officers had been killed at their posts together with most of the gunnery ratings. The final officer of the ten carried, the doctor, had died on deck attending to the wounded. Those senior ratings who had survived, including the Chief Bo'sun's Mate had been unable to get away from the places where they were marooned by the press of rescued soldiery and the bomb damage. The Engineer Officer, the Chief PO Stoker and a leading stoker were the only ones in the engine room and the signalman who had found his way to the bridge had been crouching on the deck behind the forward superstructure, escaping the blast and the splinters that had destroyed the occupants of the open bridge. Even so, it was a difficult thing to report that one of His Majesty's destroyers had been brought back to port by a renegade naval officer with an elderly retired General and one signalman on the bridge.

'He'll have to be one of ours, helping out on the civilian craft,' he declared to a surprised secretary. 'Get me the Chief of Naval Intelligence.'

A SBA brought Reissenburg back to the Captain's office together with a chit from the duty doctor in response to a query. It confirmed that 'this man has scars on his back consistent with severe lashing and overlaid by the twin flash sign of the SS.'

He had showered, shaved and breakfasted and they had given him a blue shirt and trousers and a pair of plimsolls to replace his ruined shoes. He looked a good deal better but the lingering horror and strain of the last few days still lay in his eyes. A linen sling held his arm across his chest.

Captain Brett, who had also managed to get four hours' sleep that night, greeted him, pleasantly.

'Fit to travel?' he asked. 'Commander Pallant has sent a car for you. He wants you to go to Teddington first and pick up your documents and things and then to his office. All right?'

He rose and held out a hand. 'I am glad to have met you, Leutnant Reissenburg. I shall hope to hear more of you.'

Reissenburg accept this with a wry smile. 'Thank you, Captain,' he said.

Brett watched him go in company with a seaman messenger. And what the hell can lie ahead for him, he thought.

The car was driven by an Admiralty civilian and Reissenburg relaxed in the back immersed in his own thoughts. What next? Evidently his time as a marine engineer was over. Perhaps it was back to the Tower for hijacking a RN ship, as the General had said. Poor, gallant old man, he had given his all.

They reached the house at Teddington around mid-day and Reissenburg found Ted and Rosie Brough both there. They eyed him almost with hostility as if they blamed him for surviving when the General had died. But it went deeper than that, he found as Ted came up to his room with him. He had only the small suitcase now as the bag he had taken with him from his home to Berlin was now sunk with the change of clothes, off Dunkirk.

'Did you see *Pearl Fisher* out there?' asked Ted. 'The big steam yacht, used to lie above the Weir.'

Reissenburg paused. 'Not out there,' he said. 'I saw her pass through the lock but she went downriver ahead of us.'

The man stood by the window, staring out.

'Paul went off in her,' he said, abruptly. 'They ain't come back.'

'Paul?' Reissenburg thought of the boy out there, amongst the bombing and the slaughter and the sinking ships and drowning men. 'I am sorry.'

'Paul – and the General,' said Ted.

Reissenburg shut his case. It was difficult one-handed and Ted came to help him. Their eyes met.

'I did not want to survive,' said Reissenburg, slowly.

'That's why I told the General to take you,' said Ted.

They went downstairs. 'Well,' said Rosie, in a brittle voice. 'At least we don't have to worry about him, no more. He's gone and that's it. Better than being blown up in France or shot down in a plane.' But her tortured eyes belied her defiant words and Reissenburg put down his case and, as he might have done with one of his father's villagers, put his good arm about her.

'I am so sorry,' he repeated. 'But everybody out there was so brave, so splendid. You must have pride in him.'

Suddenly she was weeping on his shoulder and Ted was muttering 'thank God.' They were the first tears she had shed.

At least he had some money on him, now, Reissenburg thought as he continued his journey. He had saved quite a bit during his employment. He told the driver to pull up at a reasonable-looking country pub and they lunched satisfactorily on cheese rolls and beer.

It was the second day of June. On the fourth day the last ship left Dunkirk and over a quarter of a million men had been saved.

11

Commander Nigel Pallant looked up expectantly as Lieutenant Jeffries brought Reiss into the room. What he saw he had not expected: a thin young man with a drawn white face and disillusioned eyes, a blue shirt and trousers with plimsolls on bare feet and a sling holding one arm across his chest – a shadow of the young man of Christmas time, physically, at any rate. Not so, he found, in spirit. He indicated a chair.

'What the devil did you mean by going to Dunkirk?' he demanded.

'I asked you for something active,' retorted Reiss. 'I went because General Carpenter asked me to go – but I did not know where.'

'I'm sorry he died. You realize you are both recommended for awards – You, particularly, since you brought *Ditchling* home.'

Reiss shook his head. 'The remains of her crew brought her home. I only pointed the way.'

'Without your knowledge they would not have got away from Dunkirk, or into Dover.'

'Of course they would. An incoming ship would have put officers aboard. I did it because the General's boat was sunk and we needed to go.' Reiss got up sharply and went to the window, staring unseeing at the Horse Guards Parade. 'I was not brave – it did not matter to die. But the men, the little boats – it was so magnificent – so terrifying. The General died for them. He wanted to go back for more. I told him we had brought them all home.'

Pallant and Jeffries exchanged a glance. Shock. What was he? Twenty-four, his first experience of war. On the wrong side, bombed and injured by his own countrymen. Struggling for his belief in an honourable Germany, freed from Nazidom, yet subjected to the full brutality of their bombing and machine-gunning of the beaches. Pallant got up and went to the window. He put a hand on the young man's shoulders and felt it quiver. He looked into the set face, into eyes dry but haunted.

'You are going back to the Tower,' he said. 'You will sleep and read and tell the Yeomen of the Guard all about Dunkirk. Your arm will be dressed daily and I'll send for you in about ten days. All right?'

'Yes, Commander. Thank you.'

Renegade though he was, he was made comfortable in his little room in the hospital wing and the Yeoman Warder who took him out to the gardens for exercise or to lie in the June sunshine by the river, was friendly. He slept, he read the books and papers they gave him and listened to the programmes they had on the radio and found himself again.

He did not speak of Dunkirk until one day when he had been there just over a week, the Yeoman, ex-Sergeant-Major, came into his room with a newspaper, open and folded.

'I asked Colonel Sherriff about this,' he said. 'He told me to ask you.'

Reiss took the paper and read the piece indicated by the Yeoman. 'Destroyer Mystery Solved. The mystery of the destroyer that came back from Dunkirk with all the officers dead or wounded was solved when it was revealed that an allied naval officer, helping to rescue troops with the 'little ships' boarded the vessel and took charge. He holds a temporary commission in the British Navy and was named as Lieut. Max Reiss, DSC, RNVR.' He handed back the paper.

'Were you at Dunkirk?'

'Yes.'

'And brought that ship back?'

'Yes.'

'Then why are you here?'

Reiss gave the ghost of a laugh. 'To keep me safe,' he said.

The Yeoman accepted that and Reiss could almost see him deciding Undercover Agent. Two days later Jeffries came to collect him.

On Pallant's desk the two-day-old newspaper lay folded.

'Have you seen this?' he asked.

'Yes, sir.'

'Well, now. You say you have broken the oath of allegiance you gave to Hitler. Will you serve us?'

'Is my oath of any value, now?'

'It can have the value you choose to give it. Now, we can let that newspaper paragraph remain just that. Or I am empowered to offer you that temporary commission in the RNVR. You would be on special duties and not unnecessarily put in a position where you might be captured by your country's forces – anyway, not without the appropriate capsule.'

'You know the Abwehr will have seen that paper?'

'Oh, yes. We hope so. We hope you may be approached now you are in a better position to supply information.'

'The special duties?'

'We might put you into Europe. A uniform would be necessary if you were not to be put up against a wall and shot. You know France has capitulated?'

'Yes. Will America come in?'

'We will tell you in due course what our line on that is. Well? Are you prepared to join us officially?' Pallant watched the struggle.

'Yes,' said Reiss, slowly. 'I will serve England in the Navy more willingly than Nazi Germany. Can I ask you a favour? Reissbaden you will attack because of the engineering works there. But I would like to think that Reissdorf could be spared.'

Pallant smiled. 'We are alone,' he said. 'Yet you talk as if we are going in and picking off targets as we like. Are you so convinced we shall prevail?'

'You must.' The tired, blue eyes were sombre. 'You must win – there is no other answer for Europe.'

'Then, we will,' said Pallant. 'I will note your request. Now – you are quite happy to keep the name you seem to have been landed with?'

'What would you suggest?' said Reiss, with a touch of sarcasm. 'Mountreissen?'

Pallant raised his eyebrows and met Jeffries' glance.

'Perhaps not,' he said, peaceably. 'Your commission, incidentally, is back-dated to first of May so that you qualify for the medal awarded for your work last month. Now, we'd better see about turning you into a British naval officer. You will be attached to HMS *Pembroke III* to learn about our funny ways.'

So Lieutenant Max Reiss, DSC, RNVR fully kitted out, found himself at RNC Greenwich and thought back to the arrogant young lieutenant in Hamburg with his long greatcoat and peaked cap bearing the eagle and swastika above the naval badge. I am still true to Germany, my Father, he thought, to our Germany. He took his cap and gloves and went down to dine in the Painted Hall.

Next day found him in a classroom with fourteen others, some foreign naval officers learning to integrate as he was, some Colonial, some newly-promoted or direct commissions from University, being lectured on Naval Customs, Defence of Ports, Chart work – by an RNR lieutenant – Censorship, Victualling, Security and all the other necessary subjects to fit them for the duties and responsibilities of an officer, which was another lecture. Reiss did not find it much different from his own naval academy work and thought with an inward smile that Baldur was probably studying the same things. It was only a three-week course, so organized PT or games were not included. Towards the end of it, one of the other foreign lieutenants, a Greek named Andros, gave him a sealed envelope.

'I was asked to give this to you by someone at the gate,' he said.

Reiss took it with a word of thanks, puzzled and opened it on his way up to his cabin. The note inside was unsigned and gave only the name of a Greenwich pub, a date and a time. It was typed as was the name on the envelope – Lt. Reiss, RNVR. He sat down on the narrow iron bed and stared at it. Who? And how did they know he was at the RNC?

The College and its magnificent buildings, the splendid Hall, the riverside, the courtyards; the ordered progress of the days, more especially the return to a service environment, had all taken on a meaning for him. What was he doing with this cloak and dagger stuff, clandestine meetings in backstreet pubs? If only he could just go back to sea... In a British uniform, in a British ship wearing the White Ensign? Or back with the eagle and swastika on his chest and cap and a ship flying the red and black ensign with the Nazi emblem?

One of his cabin mates, a RN sub-lieutenant, burst in.

'Come on, sir, smack it about!' he called, cheerfully. 'Fitness test. Shift into PT gear.' He stripped off his uniform and 'shifted' into the white, navy-edged, short-sleeved PT vest and navy shorts and Reiss followed suit. At least the vest revealed only the long scar on his upper arm. They bounced together down the stone staircase, two fit young men on a fine summer's day.

The PT Instructor, a RN lieutenant, known traditionally as Bunjy or the India Rubber Man, dressed in vest and white trousers, awaited them in the courtyard. Half the squad was standing there, the others arriving at the double, Andros and one of the Canadians revealing themselves as being sadly flabby. The PTI walked down the lines, smacking the protruding bellies and pausing to tap Reiss' arm.

'Where did you pick that up?' he asked.

'Off Dover.'

'Dunkirk?'

'Yes.'

Bunjy swung round. 'Right! Double mark time left turn double march.'

He doubled beside them to the gymnasium. A couple of doctors were sitting there, scarlet cloth between the gold rings and each man's heart-rate was checked and noted. Twenty minutes of exercises, sit-ups and press-ups followed then heart-rates were checked again and they were double-marched off to the swimming bath.

'OK. Strip off. One length, any style. Reiss come here.'

Max Reiss, reluctantly pulling his vest over his head, went. The PTI took his shoulder and turned him round and drew a deep breath.

'Don't need to ask who did that,' he said. 'They've signed their work clearly enough. All right, excused. Put your vest on. You do swim, I take it?'

12

Reiss put the typewritten note and its envelope into another envelope and posted them to Commander Pallant on his way to the rendezvous. There, he ordered a pint of mild and bitter which seemed to be the favoured brew and took it to a small table in the corner, from which he could see the bar and the door. He was intentionally some minutes ahead of the time stated. A little while later a stocky man in Southern Railway uniform came and sat down. In a conversational tone he remarked 'It's a long time since you saw Kranz.'

Reiss glanced at him but did not rise to the opening. The man added, 'You know what happened to Alec Barker?'

'Yes, I know,' said Max Reiss, shortly. 'Why have I had no contact from anyone else till now?'

The railwayman took a long drink.

'That was an oversight,' he said. 'But what the devil made you go to Dunkirk?'

'It was one way to gain credibility.'

'Well, it's certainly got you where we want you!' said the man, grinning.

'How did you know?'

'Saw the bit in the paper, of course. Couldn't believe it, at first, then we got inside information – that you were here.'

'Inside – the College?'

'I didn't say that, did I? I'm Bill Tyson. When you're posted, send me a message at the Bloomsbury Park Hotel, London. You'll be contacted.' He swallowed his drink, nodded and went.

Inside information? Reiss, taking a pull at what was not his favourite drink, wondered. Andros? Greece was neutral at present but Metaxas had had German military training.

A workman, looking at the fair young man in the grey suit, dreaming at the corner table, decided he was harmless enough and came over.

'Anyone sittin' 'ere, mate?' he asked and Reiss shook his head. 'Waitin' for call-up?'

'Merchant Navy,' said Reiss, emptied his glass and went.

The Class were called in individually and given their postings the next day. Max Reiss found he was assigned to Admiralty for Special Duties. Report to Commander Pallant RN forthwith. His cabin mates, the RN subby and the RCN lieutenant, were jubilant. They were both posted to HMS *Hood*. So Reiss packed his green fibre suitcase, officers for the use of, and his duffle bag and took a taxi to Admiralty.

Commander Nigel Pallant viewed the smart young RNVR officer, who came into the office with his cap under his arm and the two wavy gold stripes on his sleeves, with a certain grim amusement.

'Come in and sit down, Lieutenant,' he said. 'I have a very good report on you from the College. Top of the class and physically very fit.'

'The work was hardly new to me, sir.'

'True. Now, the note you sent on to me. You kept the appointment?'

'Yes. He called himself Bill Tyson and a message could be left for him at the Bloomsbury Park Hotel.'

'Do we know it, Jeff?'

'Yes, sir. Small private hotel. Letters are put on a board in the entrance hall and can be picked up at any time during the day.'

'Good. Send him a note, Max, telling him to meet you at Holborn Underground Station – now when? – Say, Wednesday at 0830. Should be quite busy, then. You can tell him where you are working and where you are living. You need to be fairly available so we'll put you in quarters at Queen Anne's Gate. Arrange with him about collecting further messages from you. In the meantime, I'm empire-building. You're joining my staff.'

'Not before time,' muttered the hard-worked Jeffries.

'Anyone question you at the College?'

'No, sir.'

Pallant grunted. 'Put Goring in a RAF Marshal's uniform and no-one would notice,' he said. 'You think we're naïve, Max? Let me tell you, just one hint that you're playing their game and you'll be in the Tower before you can blink – and it won't be the hospital wing.'

'Sir,' said Reiss, unimpressed.

However, he settled into the department well. He went with Pallant to interrogate newly arrived prisoners of war. The phony war phase had ended. Italy had entered the war in June 1940 alongside Germany. The bombing of shipping and South Coast ports in what came to be known as the Battle of Britain started in early August to be followed in early September by the bombing of London itself – which caused several Admiralty departments to remove themselves to the bunkers.

Also in August an Italian submarine sank a Greek cruiser at Tenos.

'Where the bloody hell's Tenos,' growled Pallant, searching a map.

'Kyklades,' murmured Reiss. 'South of Andros.' Andros? Why was he still suspicious of the fleshy Greek? Because he had passed the note from Tyson?

'Not the Ionian Isles? What the hell was the Eyetie doing round there?' He transferred his attention to the Aegean. 'Near Athens. I think a spot of foreign travel for you, Max.'

Reiss was not sorry. The early reports on the Battle of Britain casualties were disturbing. At first he thought the newspapers, at any rate, would be biased in Britain's favour. But interrogation of Luftwaffe prisoners told him otherwise.

His natural distress, hidden behind an impassive front, at the deaths of so many of his compatriots warred with his desire for Britain to prevail so that Hitler would be removed from power. To get away, to take part in some action, was what he wanted.

Britain had guaranteed Greece's frontiers in April, 1939 after the Italian annexation of Albania. The question now was whether or not Greece would remain neutral in the face of this latest provocation.

On Pallant's orders, Reiss informed Tyson of his journey – though not the date or the route – and asked for any possible contacts out there. A couple of days later a brief note told him 'Colonel Kyrkos.'

He embarked at Portsmouth as a supernumerary in a cruiser going out to Gibraltar and kept a low profile in the Wardroom which accepted him with some covert curiosity but no more. He had become fairly blasé, since the RNC, about his scars: after a little more than a year the lash marks had faded though the viciously scored double lightning flash was still recognizable. Perhaps it was this that made the other junior officers keeps their questions to themselves. At Gibraltar, he transferred without delay to a destroyer just departing for Malta. Here, he had instructions to find a Major Anstruther of the Royal Marines.

Anstruther, whom Reiss found in a building near the harbour of Valetta, proved to be a tall, well-built man with a bushy, bandit-like moustache, wearing somewhat scruffy khaki drill with his insignia on the shoulder-straps of his shirt. He was dark-haired and deeply tanned and could have been any age from thirty to forty. His marine cap was on his desk and he fixed Reiss with a disbelieving stare.

'Lieutenant Reiss? German?' he said.

'Yes, sir.'

'Why?'

'I found I could not serve Hitler.'

Anstruther came round the desk and stared at the ribbon on the white uniform jacket.

'Bloody hell,' he muttered. 'Where did you earn that?'

'Dunkirk.'

Anstruther shook his head in slow amazement.

'I wouldn't have believed it,' he said. 'Still, I suppose they know what they're doing. One wonders – in this mad world. Do you know what you're here for?'

'To see which way the Greeks are going to jump. And where Colonel Kyrkos stands.'

'Kyrkos? He's vaguely Monarchist. But opposed to Metaxas who became dictator with Royal consent. Both are opposed to the Communists who are anti-fascist so none of them want to join Germany and Italy.'

'Russia?'

'Not involved at present. So you want to meet all these groups?'

'Yes.'

'Right. You'd better leave your gear here. I'll draw some khaki stuff for you. Put the rank sleeves on your shoulder-straps – might save you from being shot. Just bring the Channel Isles with you – you know, Jersey, Guernsey, underwear and socks.'

Correctly relating these staccato instructions to Jersey, Guernsey, Alderney and Sark, Reiss nodded understanding.

An hour later he was walking with Anstruther down to a ramshackle jetty in a deserted cove. He had changed into the khaki shirt, trousers and desert boots that the Major had produced and sorted out and repacked his baggage under Anstruther's eye in his office. Anstruther had noted his back and said, merely, 'I think I begin to understand.' The blue sleeves with the two gold stripes were on the shoulder straps of his shirt and the small canvas bag he carried contained the prescribed naval jersey, under shorts and socks and he had a leather jacket as Anstruther had warned that the nights were getting cold.

At the jetty, an odd-looking craft awaited. Ostensibly a Greek or Cypriot fishing vessel, it had two masts but a square sail on the foremast and a fore-and-aft on the mainmast, both at present furled. It also had an ancient engine kept in immaculate order by a ruffianly-looking skipper who turned out to be a Chief ERA. The rest of the crew were a leading signalman and a couple of leading seamen.

It took them nearly a week to get to Kerkyra – as Anstruther said with a chuckle, where else would one find Colonel Kyrkos? – and to creep round its southern tip to the inlet just opposite the border between Greece and Albania.

'Remember – Greece is not at war. The Italians in Albania are,' said the Major.

Kyrkos had his headquarters in the mountains in the North of the island. He was a tall man, roughly dressed and booted, with a full beard and moustache and an uncombed tangle of hair. Despite his appearance his Greek was classical rather than colloquial and he greeted Reiss with a slightly malicious heartiness.

'They told me you would be coming to find me,' he said and sat them down and gave them retsina and proceeded to discuss the situation in Greece and Albania with extraordinary freedom.

'No, no, my young friend,' he told Reiss. 'Germany will not invade Greece, I am sure. But Italy now – ah!'

Anstruther and Reiss re-embarked and sailed quietly and unobtrusively round to Piraeus, another 370-odd miles and met there one of Papagos's officers – Alessandros Papagos being Metaxas's chief of staff. He assured them that Greece remained neutral but that any invasion would be met by the Army. The Communist leader was more difficult to find and told them nothing. On the voyage back to Malta, Anstruther asked his quiet companion 'Well, have you learned anything that I could not have told you?'

'Yes, sir, I have learned that Kyrkos is the SS Colonel Kranz.'

'Sure of that?' Anstruther was startled.

'Yes, I am sure,' said Reiss, between his teeth. 'It was he who marked me.'

13

'That,' said the Major Anstruther, talking to the NOi/c Special Operations in Malta, 'is someone you don't forget?'

'I imagine not,' said NOi/c (SO). 'Extraordinary set-up though. Well, we'll see how he makes out in *Forget–me-Not*. She's short of a watchkeeper and we're posting him to her "for the voyage".'

'To Gib. or home?'

'She's going to Plymouth for refit and re-painting, then escorting Atlantic convoys.'

'That's a job I'd not want,' said Anstruther, grimly.

The corvette, HMS *Forget-me-Not*, all two hundred feet of her, sailed from Valetta two days later. Her Captain, Lt. Cdr. Freeman RN stood on his bridge in a state of delayed shock, watching his new deck officer handling her with effortless efficiency. He thought back on the previous day's brief interview.

'When were you commissioned, Reiss?' he had asked.

'May 1st, sir.'

'What – this year?'

'Yes, sir.'

'As a lieutenant – why?'

'I had previous sea experience, sir.'

'Not Merchant Navy – you'd be RNR.'

'No, sir. Kriegsmarine.'

Freeman could picture the astounded gawp on his face.

'A – a deserter?' he had managed.

The dispassionate blue eyes had looked down at him.

'I think the word is renegade, sir.'

The Captain had pulled himself together.

'Very well, Reiss. Pull your weight here and we'll get along fine.' He had considered discussing the matter with his Number One but decided to keep it to himself and see if the man's ability justified his rank. The First Lieutenant was also a two-ring RNVR and it might be better if he did not know of his fellow-officer's history. They all knew he was foreign: his name and his accent told them that; but he could be Dutch or Danish, both countries under Nazi domination.

Freeman had handed over to the OOW as soon as they were clear of Valetta and remained on his bridge, so far perfectly satisfied. The Quartermaster had taken over from the Cox'n at the wheel and Reiss had accepted the report of the changeover with the normal 'very good' and seemed quite cognisant of naval procedure. The Captain, who had been anticipating a trip to Gib. with one watchkeeper short, felt that he could allow himself a breath of relief. The calm, rather aloof presence on watch could be quite an asset during their passage across the fringe of the Bay of Biscay.

'Where d'you go after Plymouth, do you know, Reiss?' he asked.

'Back to London, I expect, sir.'

'Special duties? Admiralty?'

'Yes.'

'A varied life. Would you rather be at sea?'

Reiss did not answer at once. 'I am still a German,' he said, at last.

'You mean you would not engage a U-boat?' They spoke quietly and Freeman did not think there was anyone within earshot.

'As an officer of this ship, I would engage a U-boat.'

Freeman drew a deep breath. 'Thank you, Reiss,' he said. 'I believe you.' All the same he hoped the man would not be tested.

The trip of something under one thousand miles to Gibraltar passed almost without incident. Some Italian fighters were seen off without damage to the ship and a sighted Italian cruiser some hundred miles off Bizerta sheered off before they were within range. They found Gibraltar picking itself up after yet another bombing raid and slipped into their berth without fuss. Reiss had sent a report to Pallant from Malta but was interviewed by an officer on the Intelligence staff. Freeman was also interviewed. He was asked if he wished to drop his replacement watchkeeper.

'No, sir,' he said. 'A very capable officer.'

'Don't forget there are U-boat bases along the French coast now,' he was reminded.

'I am quite happy,' he said.

So they began the next leg of the voyage home, some eleven hundred miles. They were about two hundred miles north of Finisterre when Freeman, snatching some sleep in his sea cabin, was awakened by the clamour of the alarm calling for action stations and the trilling of the telephone over his bunk. He snatched it up.

'Surfaced U-boat, sir. Am attacking.'

He jammed the phone back, snatched up his cap and shot up to the bridge. It was just about first light with a grey haze but he could make out the darker shape of the wallowing submarine through his binoculars. He could see small figures tumbling down from the bridge to man the *Vierling* on her deck. *Forget-me-Not* was putting on speed, reports were coming in swift succession as action stations were closed up, All guns that could be brought to bear opened up and the men on the U-boat's deck were scrambling back up the conning-tower ladder.

'She's going to dive,' muttered Freeman.

The U-boat was lying athwart their course and, bows on to her, the corvette presented the narrowest profile. As she submerged, sliding from port to starboard, Freeman ordered 'Hard at starboard' and reckoned that unless the U-boat had also altered course as she dived, he should be above her when *Forget-me-Not* had come round.

'Midships. Steady. Let go depth-charges.'

The pattern of deadly canisters flew from the stern and erupted in muffled explosions and gouts of water.

'Right, bring her round for another attack,' said Freeman, his glasses glued to his eyes as he trained them astern. The corvette swept round again in readiness for a further pattern of depth-charges. But even as she completed the turn, a vast upheaval in the water heralded the sight of the U-boat's conning tower, then the black, slimy length of her hull and then, with a great sucking and gurgling of the water, she sank out of sight. *Forget-me-Not* slowed to half-speed and passed over the spot, all eyes staring for some sign of wreckage or survivors. There was nothing and the hands began to cheer.

Freeman, with a sigh of triumph, looked round. His First Lieutenant, who had been aft at damage control, was coming back to the bridge. The officer of the watch was Lieutenant Reiss.

'Fall out action stations,' said Freeman, mechanically. 'Port watch to defence stations. Resume previous course and speed.'

He heard Reiss passing on the orders and the repetitions coming back to him. Then he turned on Number One, returning to the bridge.

'Did we have no radar warning of a surfaced U-boat?' he demanded. 'Was the sighting the first we knew of it?' He didn't know why he was angry. A successful attack despite the surprise but he felt deflated.

'No radar warning, sir,' said Number One. 'The port lookout sighted her and Lieutenant Reiss altered course to steer straight for her.'

'Intending to ram, Reiss?'

'No, sir. I knew she had time to dive. She also had time to launch a torpedo.'

'So you lessened the target? Right. Good work all round, gentleman. Now, I hope we're on an uninterrupted course for home, eh, Pilot?'

The navigator, an RNR lieutenant, nodded with a grin and bent to his ready-use chart table again. *Forget-me-Not* settled down to a steady fifteen knots, hands were piped to breakfast and the morning watch was relieved. The day's routine continued.

At 0930 on a crisp October day, HMS *Forget-me-Not* entered Devonport and secured to a jetty. Freeman sent for Reiss to come to him on the now deserted bridge.

'I would like you to know that I was happy to have you as one of my officers,' he said, rather abruptly. 'Due to your quick reaction on sighting that U-boat, we got her. One less for this old girl to meet when she goes on Atlantic convoy duty. I must apologise for suggesting you thought of ramming and admit I suspected it might have been a way of writing off *Forget-me-Not* as well.'

'I would not have wanted to be adrift in the Atlantic with a U-boat crew,' said Reiss.

'That I can understand,' said Freeman. 'You've chosen a hard path but I wish you well.' He looked out to the dockside where a couple of senior officers were approaching the brow. 'Here's your immediate boss and the Base Captain. We'll go down and receive them.'

The OOD had managed to collect a side party to pipe the Captain and the Commander aboard and he and Reiss stood back while the visitors were greeted by Freeman.

'I think, sir,' said Pallant to the Captain 'You have met Lieutenant Reiss.'

Captain Henry Hillman looked at the young man and acknowledged his smart salute. He remembered the elegant, disdainful young officer in Hamburg.

'Walk with me, Reiss,' he said, gently and they moved along the quarter-deck. Pallant and Freeman followed at a discreet distant.

'Captain Hillman's father knew Reiss's father – the Admiral,' said Pallant.

'Admiral?' said Freeman, startled. 'A German Admiral?'

'Ah! So he told you he was German. Yes – an officer of the old Imperial Fleet.' Pallant wondered what the old man would think of his son. Reiss and Captain Hillman were walking back.

'Here we are, Pallant,' said Hillman. 'You'll want to get off, I expect.'

'Yes, sir. All packed, Max? I'll hear about Greece in the car.'

Freeman and the OOD exchanged glances when they had gone.

'Greece?' said Freeman and shaking his head went below.

14

Convoys crossing the Atlantic were suffering badly. On the 18th of that month a slow one from Cape Breton was massacred by U-boat packs and even the faster ones from Halifax were not spared. Bombing of London and the South Coast continued and Reiss saw the ruined streets and wondered how Berlin and Hamburg and Wilhelmshaven fared.

On the 28th the Italians invaded Greece from Albania and, as Reiss had reported, Greece entered the war and her armies resisted and then drove back the invaders. A small British Expeditionary Force reached Greece in March, 1941 by which time the Greek army under Alessandros Papagos had occupied about a quarter of Albania. But the following month German forces attacked through Bulgaria and Yugoslavia and the county was quickly overrun. Greek guerrilla bands formed, fighting variously the Italians, the Germans and each other. By the end of April the British troops were driven out of Greece and, a month later, forced to evacuate Crete as well.

Reiss had gone back to Greece in early April but he and Anstruther got away well ahead of the troops and an MTB whipped them away to Gib. Receiving a report from there, Pallant remarked to Jeffries 'Oh, well, we should have the office boy back in a couple of weeks. I'd love to break down that "correctness" – just once.'

Jeffries grinned and shut the file he was consulting.

'Actually, sir,' he said, 'Out of the office, he's rather good value.'

'Oh? Tell me more.'

'I asked Claire – the 3/0 in the CCO – to come out but she preferred a foursome so I asked Max.'

He shook his head, 'a bad mistake: they both fell for him. Claire asked him where he came from and he told them he was a German Agent. They didn't believe him, of course. He kept us in hoots through dinner and he's damn' good on wine.'

'You amaze me.' Pallant leaned back in his chair, eyebrows raised. 'But I'm glad to hear it.'

Jeffries put the folder away in a filing cabinet and pushed shut the drawer. 'We've been to the pub occasionally with a couple of the Flags. Don't worry, sir. He's not given to fretting in his cabin with a good book.'

Reiss got back in the middle of May. He came into the office with a very smart Royal Marine officer with a neat line of moustache.

'Commander Pallant – Major Anstruther,' he said.

The Major held out his left hand, the other being heavily bandaged. 'Fell over, escaping from a pack of g'rillas,' he said. 'This fellow got me out. But they've sent me home for a bit.'

'You've been out in the Med for a long time, Major,' said Pallant.

'My second home. Have to see what the ELAS and the EAM are going to get up to next. – If I get back to Greece.' He checked his watch. 'Seeing the DNI in ten minutes. Thought I'd make my number here, though. Nice to have met you, Commander, Mr. Jeffries.' A broad smile lifted the ends of his moustache. 'Ask Max about his promotion.' He went out, his cap cradled on his injured arm and Pallant sank down on the chair behind his desk. 'All right, Max, let's have it,' he said.

Reiss had gone to the window. 'I saw Kyrkos,' he said. 'On my own. They know Anstruther is British, of course. German troops were – close. Kyrkos had become Kranz again, in SS uniform. He seemed pleased with the information I had given him last time. He said – in view of my initiative and bravery – in enemy country –' He stopped and turned to face Pallant, holding out something in his hand. 'They had awarded me this and promoted me to Kapitan-Leutnant.'

Pallant sat staring, mesmerized, at the Iron Cross on Reiss's palm. 'Congratulations,' he said, weakly.

They both saw the absurdity of it and began to laugh. Reiss closed his hand and thrust the Cross back into his pocket.

'They keep a supply of them to give out,' he said. 'Can I put up a half-stripe?'

'No, you bloody cannot!' roared Pallant. 'You've only had your commission just over a year.' He paused and considered. 'Well, not quite yet, anyway.'

'More seriously,' said Reiss and sat down on the chair in front of Pallant's desk. 'Kranz told me my brother has joined *Bismarck* and she is due to take on fuel this week.'

'M'm,' Pallant considered. 'Churchill reckons she'll wait till *Tirpitz* is ready.'

Reiss shook his head. 'She'll sail in company with *Prinz Eugen*. Räder wants her out before Hitler can stop her.'

Crete was attacked on the 20th and on the 21st the British Naval Attaché in Stockholm reported that the *Bismarck* and *Prinz Eugen* had been sighted. Together with the disastrous losses to U-boats in the Atlantic, it all made grim news.

Claire, the 3/0 WRNS in the CCO kept Pallant and his assistants up to date and looked in two days later to say that the cruisers *Suffolk* and *Norfolk* had made contact and were shadowing the two German vessels. Two days later again, she came in, shocked.

'They sank *Hood* at six o'clock this morning,' she said.

'*Hood*! Merciful God!' said Pallant. 'Any survivors?'

'Three,' she whispered and disappeared.

Pallant and Jeffries sat staring at each other. Reiss watched them. After a while he said, gently, 'You will have colleagues aboard her. I also knew two in her.'

Pallant looked at him. 'From RNC?' he said. 'It's all right, Max. We are not holding you to blame. It was a battle. You have colleagues – a brother – in *Bismarck*. God knows what the outcome will be. Many more deaths, certainly. It's all the same war. And we're both in it.'

A leading wren messenger came in with their copies of the various signals. She looked stricken but did not speak.

'Her father,' said Jeffries, 'was in *Hood*.'

There was no more to be said after that.

Contact was lost with *Bismarck* and for twenty-four hours everyone concerned sweated on the top line until a Catalina flying boat, co-piloted by a USN Ensign, reported sighting her at 1030 hours. After that, she had just another twenty-four hours to live. At 1039 on the 27th May, *Bismarck* was sunk on her first voyage by torpedoes from HMS *Dorsetshire*.

'But why?' said Pallant, fingering through the signal log. 'Why did Lutjens not finish off *Prince of Wales* when he had her?'

'Because Lutjens obeys orders,' said Reiss. 'He was sent out as a commerce raider, not to engage British capital ships, unless unavoidable. Lindemann would have fought.'

'You knew them both?'

'I had served under Lindemann. I knew of Lutjens. Hitler will not now allow any of his big ships out if there is any chance of meeting – yours. He will increase U-boat activity – and Rader will go.'

Pallant digested this, his eyes on Reiss. No-one mentioned Baldur. Survivors were still being picked up, one hundred and fifteen being the eventual count.

The majority, picked up by *Dorsetshire* and *Maori*, were landed in Scotland and sent to London for interrogation. Commander Pallant and Lieutenant Reiss went to interview some of them. It was soon evident that Midshipman Baldur von Reissenburg, aged nearly nineteen, was not among those rescued.

Then, something over six months later, Japanese bombers devastated Pearl Harbour and America was officially in the war. Wireless programmes featured military bands playing Stars & Stripes Forever, America the Brave, The Last Left on the corner, even the Radetsky March because it was by Strauss and he wasn't really German – was he? Something, anything, to lift the spirits of the beleaguered Islanders, particularly in the bombed and devastated cities, places like Liverpool and Plymouth, Portsmouth – London, where the populace trooped nightly to the air-raid shelters and the Underground Stations, emerging next morning to carry on their lives among fresh ruins.

Reiss was glad when once more he found himself on a Greek hillside with Anstruther. The Major's moustache was full-blown again and he was back in his crumpled khaki drill.

'They're putting in a small military mission next month,' he said. 'Don't ask me what for. The commie guerrillas will just take our gold and our weapons and sit tight until they can fight off the others and take over the country. They know we'll get the Jerries and the Eye-ties out for them. Oh! Sorry, old son – you trying to see Kyrkos again?'

In the event Reiss saw Kranz again twice. The first time the man was suspicious. 'Powerful forces were ready to meet *Bismarck*,' he said, looking through the smoke from his Egyptian cigarette. 'I might almost be persuaded that you are playing a double game – if I didn't know you for a pathetic little aristo who must have a uniform to parade in.'

'The British found *Bismarck* and *Prinz Eugen* in Grimstadfjord – spotted by a Spitfire. I was hardly likely to tell them with my brother aboard.'

'Why are you here now?'

'With another – to see if the ELAS will be on the side of the British when they invade next year.'

'They will invade through Greece? The ELAS will be on nobody's side. They only want to take over the country – to make it Communist.'

The second time, Kranz was more conciliatory. 'The information you gave me is confirmed by news received from another source,' he said. 'You will do well to keep faith with the Reich.'

'What a gullible lot of fools you are,' said Reiss, pleasantly. 'All the information I give you has been carefully selected by British Intelligence.'

'What?' Kranz leapt to his feet, reaching for his Luger.

Reiss shot him in the head, paused a moment to check that he was dead, then slipped silently from the deserted building where they had met. He had not gone far when a soft whistle made him whip round.

'Not what one expects from a pathetic little aristo,' said Anstruther, quietly. 'I think we'd better make tracks fast. Levkos, perhaps. I know some of the chaps there.'

'You followed me to both meetings?' said Reiss, after a while. 'Perhaps to the previous one, also?'

'You've not been at this lark as long as I have,' said the Major.

'Or perhaps I am not trusted?'

'That was not why I did it,' said Anstruther in a different tone of voice. 'I didn't want to see you in Kranz's hands again. You might have survived but I hate to think in what condition. That's why we move on tonight. We'll have the whole bloody army round here when they find him.'

'I have to thank you,' said Reiss, a little stiffly and Anstruther smiled into the darkness.

15

September, when the small British military mission was parachuted into Greece, saw their precursors embarking in a fishing boat from one of the islands of the Ionian group, not this time, unfortunately, manned by naval ratings but by guerrillas whose political affinities were somewhat ambiguous. They were preceding southwards when a couple of Italian planes heading for Sicily, decided with splendid impartiality to dispose of their bombs.

Anstruther came to his senses to find himself in the water, bits of wreckage around him and a comfortingly strong arm supporting him. He twisted his head round to see Max Reiss.

'Any others?' he croaked.

'No. They were in the wrong part of the boat.'

Anstruther accepted this and looked around. The three fishermen had been in the little wheelhouse astern. He and Reiss had been in the bows and escaped the worst of the blast. He made a mental exploration of himself and was relieved to find that he still appeared to be whole.

'You all right? You can let go –'

But Reiss was not listening. 'Engines,' he said.

Anstruther turned his head again. Distant, but approaching. British or German?

There were two of them. The leader cut his speed as he came upon the wreckage; the other sheered off and began to circle. They were British MTBs, come to investigate the bombing. Eager hands pulled the two survivors aboard, the circling boat reported nothing more sighted and they put on speed again, heading for Malta. The CO of the rescuing boat, a lieutenant commander RN came down from his bridge to see what he had gathered from the sea. They were both sitting on the deck, recovering in the September sunshine. He looked at the crown on Anstruther's shoulder-straps, the two wavy gold strips on Reiss's and squatted down beside them.

'A mixed bag,' he said. 'When you are ready, gentlemen, we'll go below and dry you out.'

'For myself, Captain,' said Anstruther, who had satisfied himself that he had no bits missing. 'I find sunbathing very pleasant. I'm Anstruther, Royal marines and this is Max Reiss.'

'How do you do, sir. You OK, Lieutenant Reiss?'

'Yes, sir.' Reiss stood up and put a hand down to Anstruther who, he suspected, was still somewhat shaky. The MTB's CO took them below. They stripped off and were given blankets and mugs of tea in the tiny wardroom.

'About six hours to Malta,' said the CO. 'I take it that's where you'd like to be dropped off?'

Anstruther, nursing his mug and beginning to lose the blue tinge under his sunburn, nodded.

'Lucky you came along,' he said.

'Yes. We thought those planes were after us and couldn't think what they were bombing here. I'll see you again later.' The CO nodded to them and went back to his bridge.

A steward brought them food and, a couple of hours later, their clothes, still warm from the pipes they had been dried on but somewhat crumpled. The boat's Number One joined them briefly while he had a meal and then the sub-lieutenant. When the CO came below again to snatch some food, Reiss was asleep and Anstruther was nodding.

'Cool customer?' said the CO and the Major glanced at the sleeper and grimaced.

'Nothing to lose but his life,' he said, 'and I don't think he puts much value on that.'

The lieutenant-commander threw them a searching glance but did not question. He had seen enough of the wreckage to recognize a Greek vessel and if it carried British officers it was fairly clear what they had been doing. The fact that they offered no explanations or reasons for their presence confirmed his belief.

They reached Valletta at 1700 hours and, after renewed thanks to their rescuers, were whipped away to see the Intelligence Officer.

He was a lieutenant commander and a stranger to both of them. He asked them morosely if they had any means of identification. When Anstruther had lucidly explained how they came to have just what they were wearing, he asked if either of them had been knocked out in the bombing. At Anstruther's admission to a period of unconsciousness he thankfully dispatched them to the Sick Quarters for clearance.

'Blow this,' said Anstruther when they had assured a not-very-interested junior MO of their well-being. 'Got any cash?'

Reiss pulled a few crumpled and sea-stained notes out of the buttoned pocket of his khaki shirt.

'Only Greek,' he said.

'Orphans of the storm,' grunted Anstruther. 'Come on. I know where we can eat.'

A Maltese fisherman's hut, where a Maltese fisherman's wife, who seemed to be very well-known to the Major, gave them a Maltese fish dish of filling proportions, washed down with local wine, was the venue. They pressed the Greek currency on her, despite her protests and strolled back to town, rumpled, unshaven and comfortably replete, where they were pounced on by a naval patrol.

'Major Anstruther, sir?' said the RPO and Mr. Rice? They're looking all over for you at the Base, sir.'

'Good,' said Anstruther. 'Perhaps somebody there will know us this time.'

Somebody did and got them sorted out, Anstruther back to his cloak and dagger and Reiss back to London, this time by courtesy of the air force. He collected his kit from Anstruther's quarters and they parted, whether or not to meet again, they did not know.

In navy-blue again, Reiss was landed at a RAF airfield after a somewhat roundabout journey and, penniless, had to cadge a travel warrant to get him to London – where, at least, some two months' pay should be awaiting him. Also, several changes.

Underground, Pallant now had two offices: an outer one occupied by two RNVR lieutenants and a WRNS third officer; an inner one divided off by glass, where he sat in four-ringed splendour at his desk from which he could observe his minions.

'Congratulations, Captain,' Reiss said as Pallant waved him to a chair.

'You, too, Commander,' grunted Pallant. 'You can put up your half-stripe. And they've given you a bar to the DSC.'

'What for?' said Reiss, startled.

'Something about sinking a U-boat,' growled Pallant and watched the blow strike home. 'You're working in here with me,' he went on. 'So you can start by telling me about Kyrkos. I gather both he and Colonel Psoros were murdered by the ELAS.'

'He said they had confirmation "from another source" that the invasion would be through Greece.' Reiss paused. 'So I told him it would be through Italy next spring.' He watched the dawning doubt, horror and incredulity on Pallant's face and added quietly, 'Then I shot him.'

'You killed him?' said Pallant when his breathing had steadied. 'Why?'

'I think he was beginning to suspect. Also –'

Pallant's dark, fierce stare fixed on him. Also,' said Pallant 'it was he who ordered you lashed – was that it?'

Reiss nodded and in his slight body Pallant saw the remembered humiliation and the resentment of generations of Counts of Reissenburg.

Glancing through the glass at the busy trio in the outer office, Reiss said, 'Has Jeffries gone?'

'Yes. He and Claire from the CCO were having dinner in a West End restaurant. It was bombed. They were both killed.'

'I am sorry. So I – replace him?'

91

'For now, yes. We may need you somewhere else, next year.'

The New Year started well for the Allies who captured Tripoli from the Germans in January and, on the last day of that month, the German 6th Army under General Paulus surrendered to the Russians at Stalingrad. Even so, Stalin was still demanding that Britain and the US opened a Second front to take the pressure off the Russian troops. Churchill wanted to strike at the 'soft underbelly of Europe' and go up the boot of Italy – reluctantly abandoning the relief of his beloved Greece – but Roosevelt wanted to invade the northern coast of France.

As the fourth summer of the war laid a hot hand on the tender beauty of spring, Captain Pallant and his assistant set out for America as part of a mission taking information and news and putting opinions and views.

They travelled in some comfort in SS *Pasteur*, one of the big passenger liners whose speed released them from the tedium of a convoy and enabled them to sail alone and unescorted. As a high proportion of their fellow-passengers were prisoners of war, they did not expect to be attacked, anyway. There were also American troops and RAF personnel. The British Navy was represented by a regular Petty Officer Telegraphist who worked in the Signal and Cipher office with two WRNS officers and three WRNS ratings and a lieutenant commander RNVR who was the Gunnery Officer and Senior DEMS man aboard. As passengers, the military mission took no part in the running of the ship, there being an OC American Troops and an RAF CO. But the two naval members were favoured and allowed access to various parts, including the bridge, the radio room and the cipher office which was just behind the bridge. Pallant noted, with cynical amusement, the rout of the WRNS by his assistant's lazily disdainful blue eyes and accented English. Why do they fall for the foreigners, he wondered. God knows, we've plenty of true Blue British heroes. What would their reaction be if they knew where Reiss came from? Mostly, it was believed that he was Scandinavian or Dutch. At least, his senior reflected, Reiss did not appear to notice his conquests, particularly.

The passage took eight days, as they left Liverpool and rounded the North of Ireland, then South down to the Azores before turning westwards for New York. They received quite a number of messages for the mission so the naval members weren't too short of opportunities to visit the radio room and the cipher office.

On the eighth day they received their berthing instructions, having passed the Statue of Liberty just before first light and preceded up river – Pier 90, South Side, was at the bottom of 50th Street, West Side, New York. The Master's Tiger found Pallant and Reiss and presented 'The Captain's compliments and would they care to go to the Upper Bridge.' The Captain, the Pilot, picked up earlier and a signalman were on the wing of the bridge and the great ship forged up river, almost past the pier, before swinging round and letting the flow of the river take her down and into the berth. The other side of the pier was empty, awaiting the *Queen Mary*, due in three days' time.

Moyra, the 2/0 WRNS found Captain Pallant, soon after docking.

'There's a message for you sir, that you and Commander Reiss will not be needed in Washington until Sunday. Remain on board.' He took the flimsy from her.

'Oh,' he said. 'That leaves us a bit adrift, doesn't it? What do you do in New York for three days?'

She grinned. 'Well, sir, we have to take the Confidential Books and waste to the BRLO in Exchange Place and get dollars from the DEMS office in Wall Street. But after that –'

'After that, you would both be ready for a drink, I expect?'

'That would be very pleasant,' she said. 'Do you know New York?'

'No,' he admitted.

'There's the Marina bar which is under the BRLO office but it gets a bit packed.' She regarded his four rings. 'I think the Astor Hotel would be a better bet.'

'If you say so,' he said. 'We'll meet you there at 1200 hours.'

16

Thereafter, they were not short of entertainment. Moyra and Joan, the 3/0, had gone on after drinks at the Astor to take the three Wren ratings out to lunch at Schrafts so, having arranged a dinner date for that evening, Pallant and Reiss remained for lunch at the hotel. On the recommendation of the ship's master, they made a reservation at the Café Arnold, near Central Park, for dinner and that night were welcomed royally by Arnold himself.

June in New York was enervating. They stayed in uniform which brought them many enquiries about England and the war. The bright lights and lack of blackout and air-raid warnings made them realize that the war had not as yet reached America. Uncertain of their length of stay, they kept their whites for Washington.

Tea with the girls at Gimbels on Friday was enhanced by details of a shopping trip undertaken in company with the three Radio officers, all solid married men, with much talk of Saks, Bests and Altmans. Since Moyra was also married and Joan was a rather serious young woman, two years younger than Reiss, these outings were all very light-hearted. Despite his seniority, Pallant was sufficiently able to relax and he had reason to recall Jeffries's remark that Reiss was 'good value'.

On Saturday night, the four of them went by invitation of the ship's master, to dine at the Louis XIV and to meet there a luminary of Radio city who took them there afterwards, going backstage with them to see the Rockettes, the famous dancing troupe, and the machinery and the sets for the shows.

In the morning, Pallant and Reiss went to La Guardia to board a ferry plane for Washington. The break, they admitted, had done them good. Now they had to get down to work.

The rest of the mission with whom they joined up again at the hotel that evening was not entirely happy. At the previous month's Trident conference, the date for Operation Overlord, as the invasion of France was to be called, had been set for 1st May, 1944 and Stalin was furious that there was to be no second front in 1943. The capture of Sicily and invasion of Italy had to be a priority. The Russian Ambassadors to London and Washington were being recalled.

The meeting recommenced at 1000 hours on the Monday morning and the members all gathered in an ante-room. There were a number of USN officers, an Admiral and two captains. One of the latter kept glancing across the room to Pallant and his assistant and Reiss realised he was the Commander from the US ship that had visited Hamburg at the end of 1938. His name he could not recall. He turned to Pallant.

'The American Captain,' he said. 'I met him with Captain Hillman before the war.'

Pallant did not look towards the Americans. 'Has he recognized you?'

'He is puzzled.'

'We'll have to play it by ear,' murmured Pallant.

There was a good deal of talk with references to BuOrd, BuNav, BuShips, Office of Strategic Services and the like which shut off sharply as the door to the inner room opened and a small, ill-looking man in a grey civilian suit stood there.

'Good morning, gentlemen. Come in, please,' he said.

The delay, Pallant assumed, as they entered the room, had been to get the President in his wheelchair into place. He greeted them, jovially, radiating great energy and Pallant recognized the almost English upper-class tones which were said to annoy many of his colleagues. As they took their places at the long table, the delegates were introduced. The American Captain was named as Captain Henry Parkin.

'Captain Pallant, Royal Navy and Lieutenant Commander Reece,' said the secretary.

Parkin looked more puzzled.

It was not a top-level conference, the Senior British member being a General, but here were certain disagreements. The British view was that the Axis should be kept busy in the Mediterranean until the Allies were ready to attack across the Channel. But the US opposed this, fearing it would take too many troops. Pallant was asked about the naval situation and was able to assure them that the Allies had control of the Med.

Knowing of Churchill's love of Greece, Roosevelt slipped in a mischievous question about the situation there.

'The British military mission found the EAM and the ELAS well established and mainly fighting other, non-communist, guerrillas,' said the General, rather stuffily.

'Are the Axis forces there convinced that invasion will be through Greece and not into Italy?' he asked and looked at Pallant.

'Yes, sir,' said Pallant. 'I understand that it has been confirmed by at least two sources.'

'What sources, Captain Pallant, do you know?' asked the President.

'Documents carried by a dead Marine officer and information passed by an Agent.'

'Passed to whom?'

Pallant exchanged a quick word with Reiss.

'To an SS Colonel Kranz – who was also known as Colonel Kyrkos.'

The President glanced at his list of names and looked up at Reiss.

'Commander Reiss. That is a very German sounding name.'

That, thought Pallant, is rich coming from one whose name is Dutch. He hoped Max would not react. He saw Parkin's gaze sharpen.

'Yes, sir,' said Reiss as if it were a remark he had heard too often.

The President did not pursue the matter and when they retired to the anteroom for a coffee break, he bade them farewell and left the rest of the discussions to the officers concerned.

Parkin, a cup of coffee in his hand, came over to the British Naval members. He introduced himself and turned to Reiss.

'Commander Reiss, haven't we met before?'

'I think not, sir.'

'In Hamburg? You're not English?'

'We have a number of officers from occupied countries in our forces, Captain,' said Pallant. 'For the sake of their families it is not always wise to use their own names.'

Parkin looked from one to the other. He nodded, slowly. 'I understand,' he said and put a finger to the blue and white ribbon with the little emblem denoting the second award. 'You're earning your keep, I see.'

The next day consisted of meetings of sub-committees, navy, army and air force, thrashing out their particular worries and on Wednesday a general meeting again to weld it altogether. The British contingent were to fly back to New York and rejoin the liner due to sail at 0800 hours on Friday but some of the senior Army and RAF officers decided to defer their departure, have a couple of days in New York and sail in the *QM* on Sunday. This would take them to Southampton instead of to Liverpool and Pallant considered the advantages or otherwise but decided that the naval members would stick to their original ship – and crew.

'Catch up on the gossip with Moyra and Joan,' he said, with a grin.

Parkin was on their flight to New York. 'My ship's in Brooklyn Navy Yard at present,' he said. 'USS *Blossburg*. Dine with me on board tonight – unless you're off to Broadway.'

'No, I'm not,' said Pallant. 'I'd be delighted to dine with you.'

'Commander Reiss?'

'Thank you, sir, with much pleasure.'

There was no shore leave for the liner's crew, the day before sailing. The WRNS officers and the PO Tel. had been into town and collected their Confidential Books from the BRLO and the latest batch of AFOs, so the office was a busy scene with the corrections being made to the CBs and the PO Tel. studying the Admiralty Fleet Orders. The naval members of the military mission would not be missed when they dined out that night.

Blossburg was an 8,000 ton cruiser with great, flaring bows, tied up to the quayside at the Navy Yard. The two British officers were piped aboard, saluted by the Officer of the Day and welcomed by the Commander who already had about four rows of medal ribbons on his tunic. Pallant managed two ribbons, a CB and a CBE as he had no wartime sea service since his appointment to the Intelligence department in London. Reiss wondered, with a certain amusement as he viewed the USN Commander's honours, what would happen if he sported the black, red and white ribbon and dangled the Iron Cross on his breast. He wore the ribbon of the DSC and bar with gratitude but felt undeserving of either.

The Commander or 'Exec' as he seemed to be called, Delaney by name, took them below to the Captain's quarters along white spacious alley-ways to a bright Captain's flat and into the large and luxurious fore cabin. *Blossburg* was very new, untainted as yet by battle.

Pallant found himself slightly relieved to find that there were to be five of them at dinner, the Americans being Parkin, his Exec and his secretary, which suggested that he did not intend to probe further into the question of the man he obviously recognized as von Reissenburg. Parkin did, however, expand quite a bit over their pre-dinner drinks, on his ship's visit to Hamburg in the December of 1938 and his and Hillman's views on the Reeperbahn.

'Ever been there, Reiss?' he asked.

'The Reeperbahn? No, sir.'

Parkin eyed him, speculatively and addressed Pallant.

'Do you know Hillman? I guess he'll be a Captain now, if he's survived.'

'Yes, he's survived so far,' said Pallant. 'He was wounded when Billericay was torpedoed and is Base Captain in Plymouth.'

'Pretty bad bombing down there, I hear,' remarked Parkin and swallowed his drink. 'Well, if you're ready, gentlemen, let's eat.'

The food was good, such as war torn England had not seen for years but the meals on the liner, which took on stores in America, were also good. Most of the conversation was between the three senior officers, Reiss and the Secretary, also a lieutenant commander, contributing mainly if addressed.

Blossburg, it came out, would be sailing for San Francisco and then to join Vice-Admiral Spruance with the Pacific Fleet.

SS *Pasteur* sailed the following morning, pulled from her berth stern-first by busy tugs, coming out into the river where ferries were crossing carrying workers and the four-funnelled *Aquitania* was going in to her berth. It was misty and promised a hot day. On the starboard bridge end stood the Skipper, the Staff Captain and the pilot and the ship was swung round to proceed downriver.

'Nothing quite like leaving port,' murmured Pallant.

'I'd prefer not to be a spectator,' said Reiss and Pallant glanced at him.

'M'm, you'd have your own command by now, I suppose.' He sighed. 'So should I. But we're just a couple of office bods – you rather less than me. Fancy Sicily, next month?'

Reiss shrugged. 'I think, sir, the Abwehr would like me to get posted to the South Coast – to monitor preparations for the invasion of France.'

Pallant was silent, watching the traffic on the Hudson. A convoy was forming up with many familiar names. *Pasteur* swept on, sounding her siren almost continuously, passing the

Statue of Liberty, swinging away to port, then dropping the pilot and off on her 3,000-odd mile journey.

17

They sighted land on the following Thursday after an
uneventful passage. Rathlin Island passed to starboard, the
Mull of Kintyre and Sanda Island to port as they entered the
North Channel; little cottages visible by the shore, rising hills,
all looking lovely.

Pallant had found that he had not been allowed to idle
during the voyage. Reiss collected radio messages and also
borrowed the AFOs from the PO Tel. so they kept themselves
up to date. On the Friday, they came to the Bar and picked up
the Pilot. Missing his assistant, Pallant went to the Radio Room
and found him drinking coffee with the 'Radio boys' and
listening to the incoming signals.

They entered harbour and tied up mid-morning on Saturday
but the arrival was something of an anti-climax, not like the
arrival in New York. The cipher staff was busy, taking
confidential books and bags of paper waste ashore. The naval
members had nothing to do but go through the disembarking
procedures, bid farewell to the Skipper and his officers and to
follow members of the mission and get a taxi, at Pier Head to
take them to the Adelphi for a belated lunch and thence to the
station for the London train.

Pallant was a confirmed bachelor with elderly parents living
in Kent. He was somewhat concerned about the proximity of
Biggin Hill but they had come through the worst of the strikes
against South-East England so, apart from telephoning them
regularly, he adopted a fatalistic attitude, as did they.

The year preceded well: The Sicily landings on July 10th
brought about the Italian capitulation on September 3rd. Also
in September, midget submarines torpedoed and severely

damaged the *Tirpitz* in her Norwegian fjord. On Boxing Day, *Scharnhorst* was pursued by British naval forces and eventually torpedoed north of the Arctic Circle by the cruiser HMS *Jamaica*. Thirty-eight of her crew of nearly two thousand were picked up.

Pallant had spent Christmas Day in Kent. He came into his outer office early on the day after Boxing Day and was surprised to see lights in his room. Through the glass he could see Reiss evidently asleep at his desk. He glanced at the Duty lieutenant.

'Commander Reiss was listening to the messages about the Scharnhorst engagement last night, sir. He's been asleep for a couple of hours.'

Pallant nodded and went into the inner office. Reiss stirred and looked up. He stood up. It was the first time any adverse news, even of *Tirpitz*, had broken down his guard, since the Plate.

'Go and shave and get some breakfast,' said Pallant, quietly.

Reiss came back half-an-hour later, groomed, washed, shaved and in control.

'I am sorry, sir,' he said. 'Admiral Bey and *Scharnhorst*. It hurts.'

'Of course it does,' said Pallant. 'It's going to get worse. Can you take it?'

'Yes, sir, I chose to give my loyalty to Britain. I don't regret.'

'Good. Because I hear there is some conflict between the Nazi party and the Wehrmacht and between Himmler and Canaris. Himmler's security service, the SD, seems set to take over the Abwehr.'

'The Abwehr is inefficient – and probably organizing underground resistance. If Himmler takes over, I shall need some convincing stuff to pass to Tyson. He will not be so easy to satisfy as Canaris.'

'They will have to give you another contact. From next month, you are on six months' secondment to Captain Hillman in Plymouth. Hillman knows who you are and can shield you if necessary.' Pallant laughed. 'You realize only about a dozen people know your identity? And they include the First Sea Lord and the Prime Minister.'

'You keep good company, sir,' murmured Reiss.

'Come off it, Max,' said Pallant, with a grin. 'Sit down and listen. We understand that von Rundstedt's view is that an invasion will take place in the Pas de Calais area. But we also hear that Rommel is being sent from Africa to take over Army Group West. Whether or not he will have a different view, we don't yet know. We must do our best to keep Pas de Calais in their minds.' He paused. 'When are you meeting Tyson?'

A few days later, Reiss in civilian suit, hatless and with his un-badged gabardine against the cold, took the Underground to Holborn. He had paused in the booking hall, looking for Tyson, when a tentative, elderly voice addressed him. 'Max? Is it you?'

He looked round and found the black-clad Jewish Rabbi, Emmanuel Levi at his elbow.

'Rabbi!' he said, startled into a smile of recognition. 'You are settled here, then?'

'Yes, I have family in London. And you are safe and well. I must go. It will not help you to be seen with me.'

'Good fortune,' said Reiss and, watching him go, saw Tyson standing near.

'Do you know that Jew?' said the railway man, accusingly.

'I have not seen him since we left the refugee ship,' said Reiss. 'I do not expect to meet him again. I go to Plymouth, next week.'

'That ought to be useful,' said Tyson. I'll let 'em know so they can get someone to contact you. Shan't see you again then, I suppose.'

Reiss left him and went back to his quarters to change into uniform. He would be sorry to leave London, he realised and the officers in the bunkers – and Pallant whom he had come to trust and with whom he felt secure. So much could change in six months. However, it was necessary to fall in as far as possible with the Abwehr's desires, more particularly now, if Heinrich Himmler, the Reichsfuhrer, had taken over from Admiral Canaris.

He left London on a wet, dull, grey, miserable day and arrived in Plymouth to find bright, clear, cold sunshine. He paused, beyond the ticket barrier, to look around. A smart seaman, with a pipe-clayed belt and gaiters, came forward and saluted. Reiss touched his cap peak in acknowledgement.

'Commander Reiss, sir?'

'Yes.'

'I'm to take you to the base, to Captain Hillman, sir.'

'Thank you.'

The parts of the city they passed through did not look too bad, despite the heavy bombing suffered. The sentry at the gates to the Base inspected his identity card and waved the car on.

The ordered activity, the briskly-moving uniformed figures, the glimpses of ships alongside, made Reiss realise what he had missed in London. It tugged at his heart. But the car swept on and pulled up outside a tall, stone building. A Wren messenger took him to Hillman's office.

Henry Hillman watched his new temporary assistant come into the office, his cap under his left arm, blond head shining. It was over three years since they had last met on *Forget-me-Not*'s quarter-deck and he saw the lines those years had etched on the man's face. He stood up and held out his hand.

'Welcome, Max,' he said. 'It's a long time.'

'Yes, sir.'

'Captain Pallant has put me in the picture. Sit down and I'll outline the duties you will have for me. You'll be living in the Officers' Quarters – a bit more in the thick of a wardroom than you are in London. Can you handle it?'

'I hope so, sir. If not, I look to you to save me from the Tower.'

Hillman laughed. He described what Reiss would be doing and, all the while, in the back of his mind lay the memory of the smooth-faced young lieutenant in his long greatcoat and the supercilious gaze from under the cap with its eagle and swastika above the naval badge.

Despite his assurance to Captain Hillman, Reiss entered the wardroom that evening, slightly warily. He had worn the uniform of a British naval officer for close on four years now and had got through, admittedly under protection to a certain extent. He refused to label himself Norwegian or Dutch, knowing full well that any native of either of those countries would soon catch him out. So he relied on the British officers' polite reluctance to pry and so far had only admitted his nationality to Anstruther and Freeman, since Dover.

The members of the wardroom noted his entry without ceasing their conversation; they noted the rings on his sleeves and the single ribbon on his breast. They noted he advanced quietly but without shrinking. A RN Commander relented and came forward, holding out his hand.

'Stowell, Mess President,' he said. 'You must be Reiss, Captain Hillman's new assistant. Where've you come from?'

'London, sir. Admiralty.'

There was a slight pause; the golden boys of Admiralty, under the notice of the Sea Lords, the Admirals and the Captains. The Commander indicated the ribbon.

'You didn't get that sitting at a desk in Admiralty.'

'Dunkirk, sir.'

'And again?'

Reiss hesitated. 'An action in *Forget-me-not*,' he said, reluctantly.

'Corvette? Yes. She was sunk in the Atlantic, I expect you know?'

'Yes, sir.'

The Commander gave him a friendly nod and left him. They went into dinner.

The Base accepted Captain Hillman's new member of staff with a shrug when it noted that he made use of the gym and the pool and walked from the Quarters to the office, usually along the dockside so he always had a good knowledge of which ships were in or entering or leaving. His ruthless efficiency did not make him popular with the many departments that he dealt with as assistant to the Base Captain and Henry Hillman recalled what Hank Parkin had told him in Hamburg: a fine officer and a bloody swine.

Commander Stowell remarked on it during a general discussion with Henry.

'Your new man certainly gets things moving, sir,' he said. 'And he doesn't exactly suffer fools gladly.'

'Not offensive, I hope?'

'No, sir. Very polite. I can't decide where he comes from. He clams up a bit if you mention it and one doesn't like to probe. He just said his country was over-run by Nazis.'

Very true, thought Henry.

'Could be Danish, Dutch, whatever,' he returned. 'Anyway, they appear to rate him quite highly in London.'

Stowell got up. 'Well, that's all, I think, sir. You've got a note of Admiral Brett's visit next week, about the landing craft?'

Henry confirmed it and the Commander left.

That month brought Allied landings in Italy at Anzio and Rommel to France to boost the aged von Rundstedt. Slowly and surely it filled the South Coast with Allied troops and strange oblong vessels. It also brought the news that the RAF dropped 2,300 tons of bombs on Berlin on the 20th.

Henry came back from lunch to find Reiss studying the newspapers. He touched him gently on the shoulder.

Rear-Admiral Brett, who had been on the staff of VA Dover at the time of Dunkirk, arrived with his Flag-lieutenant and his Secretary, Paymaster-Commander James Ruthin, the following day. Henry called in Reiss to run through the muster of troops and landing craft, which he detailed meticulously.

'The US troops will be taking part in exercises off Slapton Sands,' he said, in conclusion. Brett rubbed his nose thoughtfully as Reiss left the office.

'I suppose I started his career,' he remarked. 'You know who he is?'

'Yes, sir.' Henry glanced at the other two officers. 'I had met him before the war. We have to be a bit cagey so that we don't compromise the Admiral – his father.'

'A tricky situation,' agreed Brett. 'But I gather he's good company, eh, James?'

'Yes, sir.' James looked at Hillman. 'We saw a bit of Plymouth night life last night, sir… Reiss, Flags and myself.'

'I see. Good. It would not be easy for him to be friendly with the staff here.'

'No, sir. Friends need to know about you, don't they?'

Henry acknowledged the truth of that.

'I hear he had been recommended for another award,' he said, 'for saving some Colonel when they were bombed and sunk in the Med.'

18

The newly-promoted Lieutenant Colonel Anstruther, who knew a great deal about small boats and secret landings, arrived in Plymouth a few weeks later. Captain Pallant, also came down from London and sought permission to consult with both Anstruther and Reiss.

'Your new contact, Max,' he said. 'Who is he? Anything specific he's after?'

'He calls himself Victor,' said Reiss. 'I believe he lives and works in Devonport. At this time he wants the dates of the exercises with landing-craft at Slapton.'

'Going to call in the E-boats?' said Anstruther. 'I might be going there, myself.'

'I told him I could not get them – that the training exercises would be arranged by the Americans and, in any case, subject to weather conditions.' He paused, conscious of Pallant's dark gaze fixed on him. 'He said Captain Hillman lived at Yelverton and did I know what type of plane was at Harrowbeer.'

'Did you?' said Pallant.

'Typhoons.'

'You told him that?'

'Yes, sir. I understand they are being replaced before June by Spitfires.'

'Where did you hear that?'

'Pub talk, sir. Not from Captain Hillman.'

'Pub talk!' muttered Pallant and looked at Anstruther, who shrugged.

'I think Max is teasing you,' he said.

'A little, sir,' Reiss admitted. 'They were Czech, speaking German.'

'Merciful God,' said Pallant. 'You two know each other rather well, don't you?'

They exchanged wry smiles.

'Nights on Greek mountains, sir,' said Anstruther.

'H'm. When do you meet Victor again, Max?'

'Sunday.'

'You'd better suggest to him that these are decoys down here and the main concentration of invasion forces will be east of Lyme Regis.' Pallant looked at Anstruther. 'Any help with dates?'

The Marine Colonel shook his head. 'Any date we think might be safe will be just the one when all conditions are perfect for landing practice,' he said. 'I'd hate Max to get blamed for that sort of cock-up.'

When the cock-up occurred with the E-boats' attack and the fearful carnage among the craft and the US troops, Pallant was back in London. Reiss and Anstruther were called to Captain Hillman's office where he was alone.

'What in God's name went wrong?' asked Henry.

'I don't think they've sorted it out yet, sir,' said Anstruther. 'Some say it was friendly fire but there were E-boats there, I know.'

'It was disaster whatever caused it.' Henry looked at Reiss. 'Could they – the E-boat command – have got hold of the date, in any way?'

'Not through Max,' said Anstruther, swiftly. 'He didn't know. I'll swear to that.'

'You do not know,' said Reiss, with quiet intensity, 'what this invasion means to me. It must succeed. It must bring Hitler down. I have waited – for four years – I have worked for you – do you think I would do anything –?' He went to the window and for a moment pressed his forehead against the glass.

'No, we don't, old son,' said Anstruther. 'You've kept faith with us and look for the relief of your country. It's as much under the boot as any other.'

Henry remembered again the arrogant young leutnant zur see and his contempt and disgust for Hitler and the Nazis too freely expressed so that it had brought retribution – or had it? Was it an elaborate Abwehr plot? Could the man have done all that he had without the strength of his own conviction? He turned to look towards him and found blue eyes, not lazy, not disdainful but agonized looking for belief.

'I trust you, Max,' he said, quietly.

'Thank you. I do not betray your trust.'

Anstruther got up. 'Lunch time,' he said. 'Come on, Max. Let's see if we can eavesdrop on any more pub talk.'

In May, Montgomery came to Plymouth to boost the troops' morale. Reiss had long since seen more of Plymouth than on his first car trip through inland streets and noted the destruction of most of the city centre and the devastation wrought in Devonport. He wondered how much still stood of Berlin and hoped the SS headquarters had been wrecked.

The weeks leading up to D Day, the date of which had been fixed, were perhaps more torture to those who knew when it was than to those who continued exercises for a day which might be tomorrow – or next week. Reiss, who knew the date, could only thank God for Anstruther's support and understanding. They were both working to the limit. The deterioration in the weather on 4th of June and postponement of the next day's assault, brought dismay. A hopeful meteorological forecast and Eisenhower gave the go-ahead for the 6th. He could not have kept the already seasick troops in readiness any longer so it was either press on or call it all off for months.

Thereafter, the long-planned operation moved on inexorably. The floating harbours were ready, PLUTO, the pipeline under the ocean to feed through the necessary oil, was in place. The near-disaster at Omaha Beach was salvaged by the bombardment from the US navy.

Along the south coast of England, the furious activity paused. The camouflaged tanks that had lined suburban roads

111

were gone. The encampments of thousands of men were empty. Until the follow-up plans swung into operation, there was a lull, a chance to catch the breath, to get a second wind.

Pictures began to come back: of twelve-year-old boys in uniform in Berlin, culled from a newspaper; stories as of the three German snipers captured in Normandy who turned out to be women. All indicative of the desperate straits that fighting on two fronts was bringing the country to – or three fronts since the Italian campaign was still being fought. Reiss read the newspapers and the signal logs but showed no emotion. Anstruther departed for Otranto. Henry decided to take a couple of days leave.

Toby was away at Naval College and Anne's boarding school had not yet broken up for the summer holidays so only Jean was at home. The house at Yelverton was, fortunately, not near enough to the airfield at Harrowbeer to have been commandeered for air force personnel and Henry was able to commute unless there was a big flap on. However, the thought of two peaceful days away form the Base, was blissful.

The Base had other ideas. Henry enjoyed his first day but on the second his Secretary walked into Reiss's room with a sheaf of papers.

'Max,' he said. 'The Admiral thinks Captain Hillman should see these straight away. Are you tied up? I'd take 'em myself but I've got to get this draft ready by 1600 hours.'

Reiss got up and held out his hand. 'I can take them. Do I take the duty car?'

'Yes. I'll ring the drivers' room.'

Sitting in the back of the staff car, being driven by a young leading wren, Reiss thought there were worse ways of spending a sunny June afternoon. Once clear of the city and through the suburbs, the road traversed down land until they came to the quiet, residential area of Yelverton. There the car pulled up at the gates of two houses, separated from the next pair by their gardens and the Wren jumped out, opened the door and saluted as Reiss got out.

'It's the right-hand one, sir,' she said and he acknowledged her salute and nodded his thanks as he went up the path to the front door.

It was opened by a slim woman, perhaps a year or two older than him, wearing linen slacks and an open-necked shirt. He took off his cap and tucked it under his left arm.

'I have some papers for Captain Hillman,' he said.

'Come in,' she said and stood back. 'I'm his sister, Margaret.'

'Max Reiss,' he said, briefly and put his cap down on the hall table.

She led him through the hall and into a sun-filled room where four people sat. Henry got up, surprised.

'Commander Reiss for you, Harry,' she said.

'I am sorry, sir,' said Reiss. 'But the admiral wanted you to see these.'

'Oh, dear!' said Henry, ruefully. 'Thank you, Max. Jean, my dear, this is my assistant, Max Reiss.'

Jean had risen and came forward, holding out her hand. He took it and put it to his lips. She looked a little startled but drew him forward to introduce him to the older couple there.

'Henry's parents, Commander Reiss,' she said. 'Admiral and Mrs. Hillman.'

'Long retired,' said the Admiral, with a sigh. 'And they would not even use me on the convoys.'

'I'll just go and read through this, in the study,' said Henry. 'Stay for tea, Max.'

'I'll do it, Jean,' said Margaret. 'I'll give your little wren some in the kitchen, Commander.'

'Thank you. That would be kind.' Reiss smothered a glimmer of amusement. The little wren was called Lady Mary Parker.

'It would be very trite to say you are not English, Commander,' said the Admiral's wife, as he took the chair Jean indicated.

'By adoption only, Ma'am,' he said.

'And how do you think the Normandy landings are going?' asked the Admiral.

'Slowly, but well entrenched now, sir.'

'We seem to be overcoming the U-boat menace, too,' said the Admiral rather wistfully as if he still yearned to be a convoy Commodore. 'Have you been on the Atlantic run?'

'I have been mainly in the Mediterranean – in Greece. Once to America for a conference.'

'You've not been long in the Plymouth Command?'

'No, sir, I'm based in London.'

'He's with the Counter Intelligence bods,' said Henry, coming in with a tray. 'Only came down to us for the invasion preparations. We'll have some tea, Max and then I'll come back with you. He's been into Greece three times, Dad, to stir up the patriots and what not. But we can leave them to sort themselves out now.'

'Did you see anything of Roosevelt in America, Commander?' asked Jean as she poured tea.

'He was for about an hour at our conference.'

'Roosevelt?' said Henry, surprised. 'I didn't know you'd been to America Max.'

'I went with Captain Pallant. Captain Parkin was there, also.'

'Parkin? Hank Parkin from the US cruiser in Hamburg?' Henry glanced at his father and added 'These intelligence bods are incredibly close-mouthed. We've been working together for six months and I never knew about America.'

'Just as well, I expect,' said Admiral Hillman. 'What were your impressions of Mr. Roosevelt, Commander?'

Reiss, who had been helping Margaret hand cups and plates of sandwiches and scones, sat down again.

'A clever man,' he said, slowly. 'A devious one – and courageous.'

'To rule the country from a wheelchair? Well – he outwitted Mr. Churchill. The British Empire has gone forever.'

'If Churchill had not had to go begging for supplies, we would not have had to give up the Empire,' said Margaret, hotly.

'It was the people, I think, not the President,' said Reiss, quietly.

'Would the Americans have entered the war if the Japs had not attacked them at Pearl Harbour?' asked Jean.

'Yes. They were already committed to destroying Hitler. But they wanted to supply the means to fight and to let England and Russia do the dying.'

Henry finished his cup of tea and got up. 'I'll just change,' he said. 'Then we'll be on our way, Max.'

He came down in uniform and found Reiss and Margaret in the hall. Jean and the older Hillmans came to the door to make their farewells.

'Is Lady Mary with us, Max?' he asked.

'She is turning the car, sir.'

They left the other Hillmans exchanging looks of amused surprise.

19

At the end of June, Lieutenant Commander Max Reiss, DSC & Bar, RNVR returned to Captain Pallant's department. As he entered the inner office, Pallant looked up, leaned back in his chair and regarded him with marked disfavour.

'I have a copy of the report on your doings, from Plymouth,' he said.

Reiss paused. 'Yes, sir?' he said.

'What the flaming hell were you and Hugh Anstruther doing off Slapton Sands, chasing E-boats?'

'Chasing – E-boats – sir?'

'In a bloody little MGB?'

'Yes, sir.'

'Catch any?'

'We shot up a couple.' Reiss sat down, with a sigh. 'The shore firing was pretty fierce, though. It was a terrible mess, sir. We went back to try to pick up some of the troops.'

Pallant sat staring at him. It was four months since he had been in Plymouth and those months had taken their toll, he could see it in the man's lean, lined face and tired eyes.

'You and Anstruther and the MGB's skipper have been recommended for gongs, thoroughly undeserved for a totally irresponsible act.'

'Yes, sir.' A wry smile touched Reiss's lips. 'I was quite useful. You may recall I have some experience of marine engines in small boats?'

'Yes, damn you.' Pallant grinned. 'Talking of marine engines – has it come to your notice that a marine engineer from Devonport called Victor Hanley was found dead in a

116

ruined building a few days ago? It seems one of the walls collapsed on him.'

'No, sir, I had not heard of him.'

'Certain things found at his home suggested he might have been an enemy agent.' Reiss met his eyes but did not speak. Pallant went on, 'Tyson was killed by a train just over a month ago. You could have had nothing to do with that. But that's three – Tyson, Victor and Kranz. You are going to lie low for a bit.'

So Reiss settled back to his desk work. On July 20th came the failed assassination attempt on Hitler by the bomb planted by Colonel Count Stauffenburg. Rommel, already badly injured when his car was strafed, was implicated and forced to commit suicide. Other implicated officers were put on trial and, later, hideously executed. In November, *Tirpitz* was sunk at her moorings by the RAF, overturning and trapping her crew.

In January, Colonel Hugh Anstruther RM arrived back from Italy, wrapped up against the winter chill in his khaki greatcoat and with his moustache reduced to its military level. He came into Pallant's office, grinning broadly.

'Well, well, good morning, Commodore Sir Nigel,' he said.

Pallant's dark gaze fixed on him.

'What did you say?' he demanded.

'Oh, come on, you've seen the promotions list.'

'No, I haven't yet. I knew about the KBE but not about the Commodore.' Pallant sat back, looking pleased.

'And you, Max, my old chum – full Commander, DSO.'

'Yes,' Pallant interjected, grinning. 'They felt to make him an Officer of the British Empire would not be quite the thing.' He became serious. 'The citation, I believe, includes pulling Anstruther out of the drink as well as the gunboat chase – and the promotion is for the great work you did in Plymouth.'

'And Hugh?' asked Reiss, after a moment.

'DSO, too and full Colonel. Our gunboat skipper got a DSC. What is it, Max?'

'Publicity,' said Reiss. 'I fear for my father's safety.'

They looked at him, sobered. 'That is OK, Max,' said Pallant, softly. 'We'll look after him.'

'He's still serving?' asked Anstruther.

'When Kranz told me of Baldur, he said my father was with Group North – but that is four years ago. I have not heard since.'

'Well – I'm off to France for a week or so – be back for the Investiture! I'll ask around. What's his name, Max? I take it yours is assumed.'

'Admiral Graf Reissenburg.'

'Bloody hell,' said Anstruther, cheerfully. 'I ought to track that down easily enough.'

In February, the RAF and the USAF bombed Dresden for fourteen hours in three waves, creating flash fires and destroying the city. To many it seemed a wanton act since the war was already won.

Pallant and Reiss met up with Anstruther in the ante-room at Buckingham Palace. Pallant's elderly parents were there and Anstruther's wife and son. Reiss was, perforce, alone. Anstruther had only time for a hurried word.

'News is good, Max. We must celebrate after this.' Smart and debonair in his marine uniform, he slipped away.

Pallant, with the broad and narrow rings of Commodore, first-class, on his sleeves, went before his King to be knighted for his long and painstaking service. And, later, the renegade Kapitan Leutnant Manfred von Reissenburg, holder of the Iron Cross, first-class, stood before His Majesty King George VI and received a high award for his treachery. The King's gentle, stammering words startled him.

'We know of your father, Commander. You do him honour.'

'Sir.' Reiss stepped back, ducked his head and retired, his eyes smarting.

Anstruther grabbed his arm as he came out. 'Pallant's taking his parents home,' he said. 'I'm putting Janet and Fergus on the train for Edinburgh. Meet me in the Savoy bar at seven.' And was gone.

Reiss collected his new gold-leafed cap, gloves and greatcoat. The new ribbon was in place and the three rings on his reefer and on the greatcoat epaulettes. The order and its case he put in his pocket and the photographers and the reporters outside the Palace did not take much notice of a lone RNVR officer. He went along Birdcage Walk to his quarters at Queen Anne's Gate, not hurrying, strangely moved by the simple ceremony and the King's words, reassured by Anstruther. He had a copy of the citation and recalled bits of it. '...did save the life of a fellow officer after vessel sunk by enemy aircraft...did initiate and assist in carrying out a successful pursuit of enemy craft...'

German E-boats, manned by his own countrymen, his own colleagues. Nazi Navy with allegiance sworn to Hitler in person, not to the Reich, to the country. Had he really been justified, would he have done it but for Kranz's actions? Yes, his conscience said. It had been the Abwehr Major who had told him he was 'missing, presumed dead' and sent him to England. Never could he have been a spy, working in secret, like Tyson, like Victor, a marine engineer at the Dockyard. Yet, what had he been? What was he?

He entered the building that housed the officers' quarters. An officer just about to go out, put a hand on his shoulder.

'Congratulations, Max,' he said. 'Good show.'

Reiss went up the stairs to his cabin. He had been given the answer and it shocked him. He was a British naval officer, committed to them, proud to be one of them. He thought of Brough and his dead boy, of the old General, of Brett and his staff at Dover. Pallant and his dark stare, his offhand thoughtfulness, of Jeffries and his unhappy death; Hillman and his family, the cheerful, casual, unfailing understanding and friendship of Anstruther – with whom, thank God, he was going to celebrate this evening. They had all known he was German and had accepted and trusted him.

He looked out of the window at the fading, wintry sunlight. He thought he could be happy in England if Germany did not want him back.

Anstruther was already in the bar when Reiss got there.

'Your family safely departed?' Reiss was a little amused.

'Yes. I'm off to France again in the morning.' They took their drinks to a table in a corner. 'Jane's a fine lass and happy with her people in Edinburgh. When I'm home we can leave the laddie with them and go off on our own. And how's your love life, my old son?'

Reiss shrugged and smiled. 'Any serious attachment is hardly possible,' he pointed out.

'But you are not a dedicated bachelor like our dark-featured friend – he'll be joining us later, by the way. And, of course, you will have a title to pass on. Your father's all right, Max. He was at Lorient and was wounded in an air-raid. He had a spell in hospital and was sent home on indefinite sick leave. But they seemed to think he would make a complete recovery. Whether or not he is aware that you are alive, I don't know.'

'Perhaps, he would not want to know. Thank you for tracing him. I am glad he is home with my mother.'

'He could well be proud of you,' said Anstruther, thoughtfully. 'You have made a stand against what you felt was evil. People will not quarrel with that.' He threw off his serious mood, took a pull at his glass and said, 'Got used to the scrambled egg on your cap, yet?'

Reiss laughed. 'I can hardly believe it,' he said. 'Ah – here is our Knight.'

They celebrated well but as befitting three senior officers and dispersed not too far past midnight, Anstruther back to the hotel for an early departure that morning, Pallant back to his flat and Reiss to the Quarters.

Pallant had told them, during the evening, of certain changes that were coming. He, of course, was moving on and his replacement would shortly be taking up his duties.

'They talked of you taking over, Max,' he said. 'But I said no.' He grinned when Reiss did not react. 'I want you to come with me. So we'll all be going into Europe.'

Events were moving fast. It was some months since Cloditz had against orders, surrendered Paris intact and Pallant and Reiss went there to study and help to collate documents abandoned there and recovered by the incoming forces.

By the middle of March, the whole West bank of the Rhine was in Allied hands and on the 28th of April US troops crossed the Elbe, only 60 miles from Berlin. And Roosevelt died.

Because it was thought at first that Truman would not agree to abide by the conditions laid down at the Yalta Conference, which effectively divided Germany and Europe, the Russians made a concerted effort and entered Berlin ten days later. Mussolini was caught trying to escape to Switzerland and was executed with his mistress. Hitler married Eva Braun, appointed Donitz his successor and killed his new wife and himself on the 30th. On the 7th May, Donitz capitulated and the unconditional surrender was signed at Rheims.

Commodore Pallant and his assistant, Commander Reiss, went to Flensburg where Donitz had set up his last headquarters.

20

Flensburg and the Naval Academy were, of course, known to Reiss. Donitz had left a mass of material there, diaries of events, plans, agendas and minutes of meetings with Hitler and the other Chiefs of Staff. A collection of records from the Ministry of Armaments, in the possession of Albert Speer, was taken from him at Flensburg Castle when Donitz and his officials of the Administration and High Command were taken into custody by British troops some two weeks after the surrender. Many of the political and military leaders and their staffs were available for interrogation by the allies and many went for trial.

Personnel of the Kriegsmarine and the other services were employed on many duties, clerical and manual but all insignia were stripped from their uniforms. Reiss, encountering a cowed young man, now in charge of a stores depot, whose uniform, as shown by the darker cloth, had once borne the two rings and star of a leutnant zur See and, of course, the eagle and swastika, wondered if it had been necessary to strip all signs of rank. The Nazi insignia he could understand but did it matter if a uniform still proclaimed its wearer to have been a junior officer or a petty officer? The more senior ranks had discarded uniform altogether and lacked standing in a variety of civilian wear.

Pallant spoke fluent German but found his assistant a great help with the more technical terms and even the colloquialisms. They worked together solidly through the days and parted in the evening, the Commodore to the senior officers' accommodation and the Commander to the more lowly quarters and wardroom. They laboured there for some weeks then handed over the work of indexing and numbering and moved down to Kiel.

As troops had over-run and relieved concentration and prisoner of war camps so had more and more horrific photographs and details been published in the newspapers. Reiss studied these in silence. But documentary evidence was also being assembled for use at the trials of the major Nazi war criminals which were due to start in November at Nuremberg. The frank admissions of these atrocities, the careful lists of the names of the victims, all numbered and in alphabetical order as they had died 'of heart failure' in quick succession, brought one comment from him. He looked at Pallant and said, 'I was right, wasn't I?'

To turn against these monsters, thought Pallant: oh, yes, but – 'Would you have done it if you had not been sent to England?' he said.

It was a hot day. They were both in shirtsleeves. Reiss leaned back in his chair and frowned at the red leather bound volume on the table.

'Sir – I don't know,' he said. 'If I had not gone to Berlin, if I had just received a posting to another ship, I suppose I would have gone on serving. Kranz and Meier and what they did to me and the Jews on the ship – what we had done to them – made me decide, I suppose. I admit I felt rather sick when I gave myself up at London docks.'

'I think I suggested it was not easy to be a traitor.' Pallant spoke gently because it was not often that he found his correct assistant in a confiding mood.

'Nor is it easy to come back as a conqueror. I see them – my peers – stripped of their rank, their ships, their careers, as I was and I know their despair.' Reiss stared into the past, reliving anguish. 'But I didn't lose mine through defeat.'

'It is three months since the war in Europe finished. Do you want to go home, Max?'

'If my father rejects me –' A twisted little smile touched Reiss's lips. 'Can I become an Englishman and transfer to the RN?'

'Why not.' Pallant laughed. 'But I don't think your father will reject you.'

The door opened and their PO writer came in with mugs of coffee.

'The Yanks 'ave dropped the bomb, sir,' he said, 'on Hiroshima.'

'Thanks, Robb.' Pallant shrugged, 'I suppose it was inevitable once Suzuki rejected the terms. But God knows what's been unleashed on the world, now.'

The second bomb was dropped on Nagasaki three days later and on the 14th the war with Japan was finished. The base celebrated soberly with a cocktail party. The senior officer was a visiting Admiral and he came into the ante-room with the Commodore in Charge, followed by his Flag Lieutenant and his Secretary, both with aiguillettes on the left shoulder, the latter being a First Officer WRNS whom Reiss was startled to recognize as Margaret Hillman.

'Captain Hillman's sister,' he remarked to Pallant.

He was saved the difficulty of introducing man to woman or junior to senior officer when the Admiral, who knew them, came up.

'D'you know my Secretary, Pallant? 1/0 Hillman, You were working with her brother in Plymouth last year, Reiss.' He bustled off, leaving her with them.

'I was on leave with my parents in Tavistock, Commander Reiss and we came over to tea with Harry and Jean.'

'I am afraid I broke up the party,' he said.

'You're doing a tour of the British zone, I gather, Miss Hillman,' said Pallant.

'Not only the British zone,' she said and emptied her sherry glass with a small shudder.

'You should see what has been happening in Poland – the Germans retreating and the Russians advancing – they are as bestial as each other.' Reiss took her glass and got a refill. 'Thank you,' she said. 'Your country will be freed by now.'

'Not entirely,' he said. 'The indigenous remain.'

'But they'll be winkled out, slowly but surely,' said Pallant in a hurry.

'There are a lot of ex-navy ratings and officers here at the base,' she said. 'I see you've got German stewards, too.' She glanced at the white-coated man who had refilled her glass. 'They're so damned servile.'

'They have just suffered total defeat,' said Reiss, mildly.

'Magnanimous in victory! Good for you, sir,' she said, laughing. He smiled, excused himself and left her with Pallant.

'Henry's still at Plymouth, is he?' said Pallant.

'Yes. He was taken off the active list after Billericay was torpedoed. It left him a bit shattered. We're glad the war has finished before Toby passed out.'

'He's still a cadet, is he?'

'Yes. He's furious, of course. He was hoping to make it to the East, at least!'

Pallant continued to make small talk until the Admiral reclaimed her. He wondered what she would do when she left the WRNS. Spend her life caring for ageing parents, he supposed. A lot of people would find their busy lives at an end, now. As usual at the finish of a war the Forces would be drastically cut. It was not only the defeated who would find themselves without rank or career. He felt a slight chill as if the axe quivered above his own head. He had entered the Service as a schoolboy and had looked on it as a career for life. Now, more and more, it was becoming a service for specialists.

The Admiral departed to seek his dinner in company with the Base Commodore and Pallant decided to seek his. He could see Reiss with a couple of others, a paymaster Commander and a Commander (E) but, in any case, they would be remaining to dine in the Mess where the stewards had already laid the tables.

They met up on the way to their office the next morning and were walking down the corridor when an only too-well-

125

remembered voice said in German 'What is your name?' Reiss swing round and Pallant stopped.

'Meier,' said Reiss and the man, realizing the price of his jibe, tried to slip away. He was grasped by a large RPO and turned terrified eyes on Reiss who said, coldly, 'This man was an SS officer. Has he been screened?'

'Lock him up,' said Pallant to the RPO, 'until I've spoken to Intelligence.'

In their office, he sat down and regarded his assistant, thoughtfully.

'Well – does it all come out or do we muzzle him?' he asked.

'What he did to me was before the war,' said Reiss. 'It is what he has done since, any war crimes, he should be judged on.'

'Good.' Pallant picked up the telephone and asked for the Intelligence Officer.

Meantime, the visiting Admiral and his small staff were embarking on one of HM Ships bound for England with personnel going on leave or for demobilization. Margaret Hillman went home on a week's leave.

Autumn in Devon and the ling and gorse was out on the moor, purple and gold. Henry came over from Yelverton. He was concerned about his next posting. He had been five years at Plymouth, longer than a normal appointment.

'I met your ex-assistant in Kiel,' said Margaret as she gave him a cup of tea. 'A three-ringer now and sporting a DSO.'

'You mean Max Reiss?' said Henry. 'In Kiel, is he – with Pallant?'

'Commodore Pallant? I hadn't met him before.'

Commodore, thought Henry, with an inward sigh. Would he ever make that, now?

'He didn't seem much bothered about his country being "freed from the German jackboot",' she said. 'It was over-run by Nazis, wasn't it?'

'Yes,' said Henry, reflectively. 'Rather earlier than most. Reiss is German, Meg. He was recommended for the DSO after an E-boat incident down here.'

'German!' she said, 'Oh, God!'

'German?' said Admiral Hillman. 'In the Reserve.'

'Yes. He's the son of an old friend of yours, Admiral von Reissenburg.'

'Reissenburg's son! Fighting for England?'

'Working for England,' amended Henry. 'I think they tried to keep him out of actual sea combat. It would not have been a good outlook for him if he were captured. Not many people know his identity.'

'Reissenburg! Good God! Is the old man still alive?'

'Old man!' teased Henry. 'He'd be younger than you, Dad.'

The Admiral looked abashed. 'I suppose he would. He was a Captain when I knew him after the Great War. Very austere, upright character, strong Imperialist. He must have hated the Nazis.'

'But he went on serving them,' said Henry, dryly. 'And put his sons into their service.'

'True. But their navy was very divorced from political ideas.'

Even so, ready to mutiny, thought Henry, who had his doubts about the non-political stance of the armed forces, particularly in view of the Party Official present in most of their ships.

The terms of the Potsdam agreement signed on the 2nd of August, stating unequivocally that all armed forces in Germany were to be totally and finally abolished had reached Pallant and he passed it to Reiss without comment, watching the man's whitening face as he read it.

'Even Versailles – did not demand this,' said Reiss, at last. 'Will you be ready for another war in twenty years or is Germany to remain quite defenceless? In which case, you will defend us against Russia?'

'Us, Max?' said Pallant, gently.

'Yes. I have never denied my country.'

'No. So now, think, Max. Germany, which you won as your country, is totally devastated. Towns, cities, road, rail, seaports, factories, everything in ruins. Starvation, disease, homelessness, unemployment.'

'We will rebuild.'

'What with?'

Reiss was silent for a while and his thoughts were obviously not to his liking. He sighed deeply.

'American aid,' he said. 'You gave all your dollar reserves, even your Empire for their aid to fight this war. They let you and Russia fight Hitler and they have taken his dream to rule the world.'

'Maybe, but do you realise what it's going to cost them? Those terms – that's the voice of retribution. The voice of reason must follow. We cannot have you sitting here between Russia and France, totally helpless.'

'Thank God their aid will be of necessity and not charity,' said Reiss, bitterly.

21

Commodore Crowhurst strolled into the office a day or two after the discussion between Pallant and Reiss, regarded their book and paper-strewn table with interest and took a chair opposite Pallant.

'I understand that one of the German staff was denounced as an ex-SS man and locked up for further investigation, Nigel,' he said.

'Yes. He's gone to Flensburg, I believe, to be vetted.'

'I would not have taken particular notice of it,' said Crowhurst, almost apologetically. 'Except that I have had a communication from the military Commander at Reissbaden.' He looked blandly from Pallant to Reiss and back again. 'He says that the principal landowner there – who is Count Reissenburg – was informed by this man, Meier, that the Count's son who was reported as missing, presumed dead, from his ship in 1939 was in actual fact sent to England as a refugee from the Nazis, to act as a – ah – secret agent and that he is here in Kiel masquerading as a naval officer under the name of Max Reiss.'

Pallant and Reiss exchanged an amused glance.

'Not masquerading, Phil.' said Pallant. 'He gave himself up to us as truly a refugee from the Nazis and has done a great deal of good work for us.'

'A turncoat?' said Crowhurst in gentle disbelief.

'A turncoat, a renegade, a traitor, whatever you like, sir,' said Reiss. 'Or – perhaps – just an anti-Nazi?'

'Yes. Well, you chose a better way of showing it than those poor devils who tried to assassinate Hitler.' His eyes rested on Reiss's ribbons. 'I don't suppose you got those for nothing. I'm glad to know the truth of it. Your father, Reiss, said that he would like to know if you were alive but, if you had been a Nazi spy, he had no desire to see you.'

Pallant and Reiss started to laugh and Crowhurst watched them, tolerantly.

'He would have put you in the soup if you had been, Max,' chuckled Pallant, 'with every chance of being shot at dawn.'

'Probably his intention,' said Reiss, with sad understanding. 'To him, a spy is without honour and better dead.'

'And he would know that Meier would give you away?' said Crowhurst. 'You may have to go to Flensburg if there is a tribunal?'

'I think we can put the stopper on that,' said Pallant. 'We prefer to keep our activities quiet, you know, Phil.'

'So I believe. Well, I think you'd both better consider a trip to Reissbaden. I gather the Count has some documents from Lorient that might be of interest.' He got up. 'Good luck, Commander. I compliment you on what you are doing.'

'Thank you, sir.' Reiss sat down again as Crowhurst left and Pallant thought he seemed rather downcast.

'We'll amend our itinerary,' he said. 'Hamburg next, then we'll fit in a day or two at Reissbaden; Frankfurt and then this castle near Coburg. I gather there are about sixty thousand files there but, thank goodness, not too many will concern us. Then we should fetch up at Nurnburg in November.' He turned his dark gaze on Reiss. 'Are you scared about going to Reissbaden?'

'No, sir.'

The flat reply made Pallant laugh. 'Well, at least you'll know whether you're going to be the next Graf or a naturalized Englishman!' he said and elicited a rueful smile.

They proceeded a few days later, in their car with the PO writer and German driver, to Hamburg where they had only to collect and check over some material already collated for them. This boxed, sealed and left ready for transport later to Nurnburg, they went on to Reissbaden and pulled up in the

130

town square outside the Military Commander's commandeered premises. The Commander was a cheerful Royal Engineers Major and his second in Command was an RAOC Captain. Between them, it seemed they had the little town nicely buttoned-up and were getting essential supplies well-organized and the marine works up and running again, making components and accessories.

It was a pleasant, slightly autumnal day at the beginning of September and Reissbaden was relatively undamaged and looking very nearly its best. The RE Major Bailey had the Lorient papers in his safe and on going through them, Pallant decided to take them with him to Nurnberg or possibly to have them boxed at Coburg, depending on what was there.

'Will you and Commander Rice be staying overnight, Commodore?' asked Bailey. 'Be better to start for Frankfurt in the morning.' He looked out at the afternoon sunshine and sent for tea. He and the Captain were evidently appreciative of visitors from England.

'I would like to have a chat with the Count before we go,' said Pallant, mildly. 'Being naval – how do you get on?'

'Oh, he's very co-operative. The machine factory is his, of course. He's rather waiting for –' He stopped suddenly and put his cup down in its saucer abruptly.

'Commander – Reiss,' he said. 'Max Reiss? My God!' He grinned. 'That's not playing fair, sir. Will you go up to the Schloss or shall I ask him to come here?'

'I think we'll go up – eh, Max? We might get a bed for the night!'

'I'll give him a ring,' said Bailey and picked up his telephone. 'Connect me to Reissdorf, please. Herr Graf, can you receive Commodore Pallant of Naval Intelligence and Commander Reiss, now?' He listened for a moment. 'Thank you, sir.' He put down the receiver. 'He hopes you will accept his hospitality for the duration of your stay here.'

Outside, Pallant paused by the car.

'Sure you don't want to go on your own? I can follow,' he said.

'Of course not!' The aloof blue eyes were amused. 'My father would be very upset. Please do not think you are going to witness the return of the Prodigal.'

Pallant shrugged, grinned and got into the car.

The Schloss, with the small village clustered outside its gates, was fairly modest compared to the Rhineland castles. The car was met at the foot of the steps leading to the main entrance by an elderly, black-suited manservant.

'Direct the driver, please, Josef,' said Reiss and laid a hand briefly on the man's shoulder. 'Come, sir.'

The Admiral was awaiting them in the hall, upright, austere, feet apart and hands behind his back as he might have stood on his bridge. His eyes went directly to his son, to the uniform, the wavy gold rings and the ribbons. But only momentarily. He came forward to greet Pallant.

'Commodore, it is a great pleasure,' he said in clipped, precise English. They shook hands and then he held out his hand to Reiss, who took it, bowing his head. 'My son, would they not take you in the Royal Navy? They took Louis and Philip.'

'I think the Reissenburgs are not so well connected as the Battenburgs, my father.' There was a quiver of laugher in his voice and the Admiral smiled and nodded and turned back to Pallant.

'You are able to stay, Sir Nigel? Joseph will show you your room. Manfred, your mother awaits you.'

An hour or so later, Pallant had emerged from the bath Josef had run for him and was dressing in the adjoining bedroom, in the freshly-pressed uniform and clean underpants, socks and shirt taken from his case and laid out on the bed for him. A tap on the door heralded his assistant, looking fresh and spruce.

'Has Josef seen to everything, sir?' He cast a searching look around the room. 'I gather the food situation has been bad for

132

the last year or two but is better now. Of course, we are not short of help. Those who have returned to the village need work. I am glad the factory is in production again.'

Pallant, knotting his tie, watched him in the looking-glass, a lean-faced man, thinking of his family's dependants and remembered the smooth-faced 23-year-old in the creased grey suit of six years ago, whom he had sent to work in a riverside boatyard.

'You've seen a lot since you were last here, Max,' he said. 'Look, I can expedite your demob, if you want.'

'Oh, no, please! I wish to carry on as long as possible. Certainly to Nurnberg and as long as I may be useful. To go to sea again would be wonderful. But the RN, of course, was just a dream.'

'Another ten years, Max – you won't be too old to command a flotilla or something.'

'In ten years - you think we will have ships again?'

'Ten to fifteen years, I reckon you'll have a navy again. Right, I am ready. What next?'

'We will join my father for a drink before dinner.'

The Admiral was still in his dark suit as Pallant had no dress clothes. The Grafin was also in a day dress and Pallant was presented to her.

'I understand Manfred was given his medal by your King,' she remarked. 'We are distantly related – through the House of Teck, of course, not Saxe-Coberg. But he does not tell me what he received it for.'

Pallant glanced at the impassive-face recipient.

'No, Grafin,' he said. 'It was what we call "hush-hush".' He thought Reiss had probably not wished to tell his mother he had been bathing in the Med supporting an unconscious colleague – or that they had been chasing E-boats together later.

The fatted calf was not killed but they dined simply on soup and a fine veal dish which made Pallant smile, followed by some sort of torte. The Admiral spoke a little of his wartime service and Pallant asked if they could go through the Lorient diaries together the next morning.

'It is Sunday tomorrow,' said the Admiral. 'Will you attend church with us? Then I am at your disposal.'

Pallant hesitated. 'Admiral, there are some even here who might wish to harm your son.'

'He must come to accept that some will call him traitor,' said the Admiral, calmly. 'I accept that he fought against Hitler and not against his country. Perhaps many more of us should have done so. But I doubt if even history will ever explain the thrall in which Germany was held – for a great part willingly, I know. Even Donitz revered Hitler to the end.'

'We will attend church with you, tomorrow, sir,' said Pallant.

When they went up to bed, Reiss offered Pallant a nightcap and took him to his own apartments. Pallant, subsiding into a deep armchair and accepting a whisky, viewed the large and comfortable room and wondered again what the complete loss of life as he had known it, had cost the man. From his ship to a refugee vessel; from this home to the Broughs'. From a promising career to a very uncertain future. All for a few indiscreet words.

'I think we were unpopular,' said Reiss, as if reading his thoughts. 'You noticed that my father was never given a sea-going command? It hurt him, I think. He was experienced – he could have commanded a battle fleet.'

'At least he survived,' pointed out Pallant. 'I expect he will want to know more about you. How much do you want him to know?'

Reiss shrugged. 'What ever is permissible? He will not try to pump you.'

'Good.' Pallant finished his drink and stood up. 'Thank you, that was fine. I am ready for a good sleep now. Please see I am up in time for church parade!'

22

The 'church parade' passed off without incident and it was evident that the Graf was a respected landlord; on his son, Pallant felt, the villagers were reserving judgment. Whether or not they recognized the wavy stripes on his sleeves, the Royal Navy cap badge was obviously the same as worn by his senior officer. Some murmured their pleasure that he was safely home. The memory of young Baldur, whose photograph Pallant had seen in the house, was certainly present.

They returned from the little church to coffee and cakes, served by Josef and afterwards Pallant fetched his briefcase and produced the Lorient papers. They recorded the sailings, returns or losses and details of the sinking made by the U-boats over the two years that the Admiral had been there. When they had been through them, as Pallant had expected, the Admiral asked mildly if he could be told something of 'Max Reiss's' activities. He visibly bristled when he heard of the SS treatment – a somewhat expurgated version – and eyed his son with sharpened interest when he spoke of the Jews and their resilience in the refugee ship. Pallant took up the story and noted the Admiral's grim appreciation of the engineering apprenticeship served and the 'little ships' at Dunkirk. The saga of the damaged destroyer Ditchling and the subsequent offer of the temporary commission made him nod understandingly. Pallant skated over the Greek episodes, expanded on the visit to America and was diplomatic over the invasion preparations.

'Since then, sir,' he concluded. 'We have been collecting and sorting material for presentation at the War Crimes tribunals.'

The Admiral rang for pre-lunch drinks. 'You have had an interesting war, Manfred,' he observed. 'What next?'

'If I am not needed here, sir, I will go on until I am thrown out.'

'And then you can come and run the machine works at Reissbaden. But I don't know if it will be marine engines.'

They exchanged ruefully amused glances and Pallant realised that father and son were far more in tune than he had expected. He accepted a fine dry sherry from Josef and wondered how the Graf had kept up his cellar. They all rose to their feet as the Grafin came in to join them.

'The Grafin asks that you will remain another night. I hope you will be able to do so, Commodore,' said the Graf.

'That is very kind,' said Pallant. 'Yes, indeed. But tomorrow we must get to Frankfurt.'

'Frankfurt? That is in the American zone. About two hundred – two hundred and forty kilometres, I suppose. You will do that comfortably – if the roads are not too bad.'

They departed after breakfast the next day. Their driver, who with the PO Writer, appeared to have no complaints about their entertainment, stowed their cases and they made their first stop in Reissbaden to check out with Major Bailey. It was here that, as they got out of the car, a man leapt forward, shouting 'traitor' and stabbed at Reiss with a knife. Pallant, swinging round, did not see exactly what happened. Reiss caught hold of the hand with the knife, twisted the man round and chopped the side of his neck with his other hand. The sentry on the door of the Command HQ, who had jumped forward, pulling his revolver from its holster, stopped abruptly as the assailant flopped lifeless into the gutter.

'Gawd, sir, where'd you learn that?' he said.

Which was what Bailey asked. 'You've saved us a trial, I suppose, Commander,' he said. 'That was a commando trick, surely.'

'Yes. I was taught by a Colonel in Greece,' said Reiss. 'We found it quite useful, once or twice.'

Pallant raised metaphorical eyebrows. Evidently, reports from Anstruther and Reiss had not been as detailed as they might have been.

'You meant to kill him, Max?' he said.

'Yes,' said Reiss, reluctantly. 'He was Nazi. He was employed at the machine works, a trouble-maker.'

'Ah,' said Bailey, with satisfaction. 'We had our suspicions. So he spent the war here and not in the services?'

Reiss shrugged. 'He was certainly here when I left in 1939.'

'Can you deal with it, Bailey?' asked Pallant. 'We must be on our way. You won't want Max for an inquest or enquiry?'

'No, sir, I think we can sweep it under the carpet,' said Bailey, cheerfully. 'It's not the first incident – and it won't be the last, I'm sure.'

Frankfurt was reached in time for a late lunch at the US officers' club to which Commander Delaney, who welcomed them, took them. It seemed to cater for commanders and upwards, unlike the British wardroom which cut off at commanders. As Pallant remarked later, if your cap has scrambled egg on it, you're in. Although speech, uniforms and attitudes seemed to the two incomers to be sloppy, the deference given to flag rank was marked. Delaney re-introduced himself as having been Exec. in USS *Blossberg* when Captain Hank Parkin had brought them aboard in Brooklyn Navy Yard.

'No, we lost Hank Parkin last year when *Blossberg* was sunk off the Philippines,' he said in response to Pallant's enquiry. 'A fine man. No, Commodore, I don't know that we got a lot for you here, navy-wise. A great deal on the German war economy and the impact our bombing had. Albert Speer's reports, of course. But they won't be in your remit. Anyway, we got plenty to nail these krauts at Nuremburg and nail 'em we must or another twenty years or so they'll be at it again, make no mistake about that. It's a trial of war criminals and criminals they are and must be hung like those poor buggers

137

who tried to stop Hitler. You'll find more of what you want at Schloss Tarnbach.'

Reiss made no reference to Delaney's krauts at Nuremberg speech until a week or so later when they were at Coburg. He lifted his head from the Donitz diary he was perusing, leaned back in his chair and looked at Pallant.

'Do you think, in twenty years or so, when I am commanding my destroyer flotilla, I shall be "at it" again? I don't think world domination will come by war.'

Pallant sat up, his dark eyes alert. 'But you think world domination is still a goal?'

'The US is near to it. The British would have had it if your German king had not lost the American colonies. The Empire was worldwide.'

'And coveted.'

Reiss smiled. He looked weary. 'That was not really what I wanted to speak of.'

'No. It was nailing the krauts at Nurnberg, wasn't it?'

The smile was bleak. 'Krauts – Boche, Hun, Fritz, Jerry – what do names matter? But – a tribunal is a court of justice. I do not see justice at Nurnberg. Retribution, yes. But Hitler is dead. I understand the trial of Goring, Goebbels, Himmler. But the Service chiefs who had to carry out their orders? Would you have indicted Rommel – whom you admired – if he had not been forced to suicide? Why Rader, who resigned when Hitler wished to destroy the big ships? Why Donitz who was a U-boat man and did not ask to succeed as fuhrer? Surely not because his U-boats were so successful?'

Pallant sighed. 'Donitz, I don't know what the indictment is. Rader, I am told, for the invasion of Norway. As you say, they were carrying out orders. I am not sure about these trials. As Churchill said, insofar as I remember, 'It would be little use punishing the Hitlerites if law and justice did not rule: we must be worthy of the immense forces that we wield. But I doubt if Truman and Stalin have the same sort of wisdom.'

'Nor Attlee for whom you have thrown out Churchill?'

138

Nurnberg had been raided by some eight hundred aircraft on the last days of March, 1944 and not much was left standing. The courthouse where preparations for the trials were being made and some buildings to house those who had to be there. It was here that Colonel Anstruther caught up with them.

'Here, come on,' he said. 'There are still some rooms free in my quarters. Anyway, I'm not staying for the trials.'

'Why are you here?' asked Pallant.

'As you know, I've been in France,' said Anstruther. 'I've only just heard that some of our chaps were murdered in Greece, last year. I came here to see if I could find out who were the German Intelligence officers at the time.'

They were in his room in the commandeered hotel, drinking whisky, Pallant relaxed in the armchair, Anstruther sprawled on the bed and Reiss on the upright chair by the table. 'Any luck?' said Pallant.

'No. So I'm off to Greece next week. Commodore, will you lend me your assistant?'

Pallant smiled, swirling the liquid in his glass.

'I'm glad you asked,' he said. 'I was considering sending Max home.' His smile broadened as Reiss looked up in protest. 'Max,' he went on, gently, 'you've not faltered. But it is bad enough for me reading these documents and the people concerned are nothing to me. For you – I cannot imagine.'

'Gave me a shock when I saw you,' affirmed Anstruther. 'Not my bright-eyed, bushy-tailed companion of the mountains. Come on, old son, these revelations are cutting you up. A nice sea voyage will put the colour back in your cheeks.'

Reiss was silent for a moment, Anstruther's last comment bringing a wry amusement to his lips. Then he drew a long, shaky breath. 'Thank you,' he said. 'I think – I could not have faced the trials. The shame of my country... I find I am still very much a German.'

'Good,' said Pallant. 'Germany will need you when all this is over.'

Anstruther had secured passage in a cruiser, HMS *Monsarrat*, which was going to Greece to link up with a military mission there. She was lying at the docks in Hamburg and he and Reiss were flown from Nurnberg to the ex-Luftwaffe airfield there to join her. Anstruther was amused over something which he did not impart until they were arriving.

'I'd better warn you, Max,' he said. 'The Captain is a xenophobic Welshman. He thinks the RNVR is a yachting club.'

'Even after six years of war? Well – I should not come to his notice very much.'

The ship, going on a peacetime mission and with many Reservists being demobilized, was not fully staffed and there was no trouble in allotting cabins to the passengers. They were both put in the officers' cabin flat which also housed the Pilot, Guns, Torps, the Paymasters and Doctors, the Chaplain and the Captain of the small Marine contingent aboard. Being equal in rank to a naval captain, Colonel Anstruther was not strictly a wardroom officer. However as he was taking passage for the voyage only and had no active duty it was more convenient for him to mess there. The RM Captain quickly made himself known and they happily settled into service chat over a pre-lunch drink.

During the orderly bustle of departure the passengers kept themselves out of the way, finding a sheltered spot on the quarterdeck to watch the ruins of Hamburg drop away. It was cold and the aspect was grey. Anstruther had on his heavy greatcoat and Reiss a thick bridge coat. When they saw the Captain descend from his bridge and go below they decided the warmth of the wardroom called. However, as they descended the companionway, a Paymaster lieutenant commander met them.

'Colonel Anstruther? Commander Reiss?' he said. 'The captain's compliments, sir. He would like to see you both in his cabin.'

Captain 'Dai' Williams, DSO, RN was short, slight, dark and dapper. He greeted them as they entered his fore cabin and his secretary hung their coats and caps in the lobby.

'I'm not used to carrying passengers aboard my ship,' he remarked as they sat down and his steward brought coffee. 'But you're very welcome.'

'We're willing to work our passage, Captain,' said Anstruther.

'Well, I don't know what you can do with the Marines, Colonel,' said 'Dai'. 'But I might need the Commander here. How's your navigation, Reiss – You're Intelligence, I believe.'

'Yes sir. But if you need a navigator, I can do it.'

The Captain shot a glance at him: his accent was slight now but it was still there, more so since recently he had been using his own tongue more frequently.

'I think the Pilot's going down with flu,' said the Captain. 'He was pretty groggy just now. Should be all right for the moment, down the river.'

Reiss put his cup down. 'Sir, I am familiar with the Elbe. If your officer has flu, I'd feel safer if he were in bed.'

Anstruther chuckled. 'Let him go, Captain,' he said. 'He hates being idle.'

Williams looked from one to the other. 'All right,' he said. 'I'll ring the bridge and say you are relieving him and he is to report sick.' He took up his telephone as Reiss collected his coat and cap and went out. 'If I'd known I'd have left him in Hamburg – Bridge? Captain here.'

Having dealt with that, he appeared to have qualms.

'Is Commander Reiss an efficient pilot, would you say, Colonel?'

'Oh, yes, very.' Anstruther was enjoying himself.

'What is he? South African? Can't be. Too correct. Dutch?'

'No, he's pure German.'

There was a fraught silence. 'You mean I have sent a German naval officer to my bridge?' croaked 'Dai'. 'But he had British medals and service ribbons. I don't understand.'

So Anstruther told him.

23

On the bridge, the Officer of the Watch greeted Reiss's arrival. He was a lieutenant commander RN and he noted the three wavy stripes on the shoulder straps of Reiss's coat.

'I understand you're taking over from the Pilot – sir,' he said. 'He's in the chartroom.'

Reiss nodded. In the chartroom, he found another RN two-and-a-half-ringer, attended by his assistant, a midshipman RN. The pilot, who was bowed over the chart table raised haggard eyes to look at his relief.

'Do you know this bloody river – sir?' he asked, thickly. 'I think we've got all the wrecks marked on the chart.'

'I should hope so, after six months,' said Reiss, crisply and the Pilot stiffened.

'Sorry sir. This is Midshipman Fielding. He'll fill you in. Orders are here. I've marked the course from Cuxhaven.' He was swaying on his feet.

'Cut along, Pilot,' said Reiss. 'I'm only here until you're better.'

The man managed a grin. 'Thank you, sir. I'll go and find the PMO. Tanky knows the ropes.' He lurched out.

'What's she drawing, Mr. Fielding?' asked Reiss.

The lad, a smart looking youngster, appeared to share his Captain's opinion of the 'Wavy Navy' as weekend yachtsmen. He had, most probably, not left training college by the end of the war, when so many of the amateur sailors who had outnumbered the regulars by then, were being de-mobbed.

'It's logged, sir,' he said.

'I'm sure it is,' said Reiss, mildly, studying the charts. 'Don't you know?'

The boy, compressing his lips, read the ship's draught from the log. He told a furious and uncomplimentary tale when he got to the Gunroom, later.

The ship was proceeding quietly; where they were at that moment the river was broad and they had about fifty miles to go. Reiss watched some small islands on their starboard side. He could remember the great Hamburg-Amerika liners passing down this way, to cross the Atlantic. He had seen the Bremen come in to dock on her last trip back from New York. All that had gone – forever, he feared. He went out to the bridge and checked the ready-to-use chart there. A small, dapper figure appeared and nodded to the OOW.

'All right, Commander Reiss?' he said, sharply.

The years of training, the return to the bridge of a warship, worked. Reiss, turning from the chart, came to attention.

'Yes, sir,' he said.

Captain Williams looked him over, obviously finding him a new specimen in the light of Anstruther's revelations.

'Good,' he said. 'The Pilot's pretty sick. We may have to land him. You know the way into Wilhelmshaven, I don't doubt.'

'Yes, sir.'

'Useful!' 'Dai' smiled tightly and went out.

The OOW, Commander (E), who had come up since his engines were only at half-speed, the Signals Officer and the sub-lieutenant of the watch, all glanced at their stand-in pilot with varying degrees of curiosity but no-one put a question. Reiss, totally amused at this display of British reticence, went back to his charts.

By 1930 hours the ship had left Cuxhaven behind on her port quarter and was heading out into a turbulent North Sea. With course and speed hopefully constant for the next couple of hours and a competent watch keeper on the bridge, Reiss decided to go below for dinner. He had a quick shower, in company with the First Lieutenant under the next one, found a clean shirt and arrived at the wardroom ante-room at the same

144

time as the Number One. They entered just in time to hear the officer who had stood the afternoon watch say mockingly 'The Old Man asked if he was OK and he almost clicked his heels like a ruddy kraut.'

The last words fell into a slight hush as others saw who was coming in. The speaker turned, disconcerted. Reiss looked at Anstruther who, he was pretty certain, had put the Captain wise.

'But I am a ruddy kraut,' he said.

Encouraged by the amusement apparent in his voice, the speaker said, 'Just a turn of phrase, sir – nothing personal.'

Anstruther got up. 'He's been with naval intelligence for the past six years,' he said. 'And as you know us bods are rather shy. Just for your ears, though, some of our SBS Commandos were murdered in Greece last year and we're going to see if we can find out who did it. Drink Max?'

Reiss glanced at the whisky glass in the Colonel's hand. 'Evian, sir, please,' he said. 'I may be driving tonight – if the Captain wants to get into Wilhelmshaven.'

'Tell me, sir,' said Number One. 'Would the fact that the SS have left their brand on your back, have anything to do with your career?'

'Everything. Before that, I was lieutenant in the Kriegsmarine.'

'Thank God for that,' drawled the Engineer Commander. 'I now have complete confidence in your navigation.'

The Captain did not want to put into Wilhelmshaven as the PMO decided to keep the Pilot in his own care and jocularly suggested that a Mediterranean cruise might be beneficial. Even so, Reiss went back to the bridge a couple of hours later and checked the ship's new course. It was a clear, cold night and he felt at peace. Except for his name he was now out in the open and, seemingly, acceptable for what he was. How much Anstruther had disclosed he did not know – the nights on Greek mountains were conducive to confidences and they probably knew as much about each other as any man could know of another. He thanked God that the Colonel had rescued him from the Nurnberg documents and brought him back to sea. Another three-fifty miles to the Dover Strait, roughly mid-morning, then two-and-a-half thousand or so to Greece. If they managed to keep up to six hundred miles a day with probably calls at Gibraltar and Malta, they would be there within the week. He did not bother to establish exactly the course he had plotted but the speed and the port calls were up to the Captain.

He was still dreaming, looking out of the forward screens, when the First Lieutenant came up to take the Middle Watch at midnight. He listened while they handed over and then the Number One came towards him.

'Commander Reiss,' he said. 'I hope I didn't speak out of turn in mentioning the scars on your back. When I saw them in the shower, I couldn't believe – I thought that sort of thing belonged to the Middle Ages.'

'Did you?' Reiss regarded him, speculatively in the dim light. 'Even your people were disembowelling traitors later than that. Can you believe that it is all still happening now, in Poland, in Russia, in Greece where I am going with the Colonel?'

'Yes.' Number One gave a grunt of annoyance. 'Of course I believe it. Of course I know about the death camps still in Russia. I know unspeakable things are done in Third World countries. I had not come face to face with it, before.' He gave a short laugh and added, 'So to speak!'

'But we all ignore those things – that we don't come face to face with – because trade figures and international relations are so much more important. Goodnight, Number One.' Reiss touched his cap to acknowledge the First Lieutenant's salute and went to the Navigator's sea cabin.

Captain Williams came into the chartroom in the morning as they entered Dover Strait.

'Morning,' he said. 'Look, Reiss, I can signal Plymouth to find me a navigating officer if you wish. We're not due for a port call there and they'll want me to land Johnnie…'

'If you are content, sir, I am willing to carry on.'

'Good!' Dai looked relieved. 'The Pilot should be fit before we're due to return and I'd prefer to keep him on board. Have you been this way before?'

'In reverse, sir. From Malta to Devonport in a corvette, as a watchkeeper, and as a passenger from Portsmouth to Malta.'

'Stepping stone for Greece? And you're going back to find the bastards who executed our commandos?'

'Yes, sir.'

'H'm. Partisans?'

'Probably SS. Colonel Anstruther wants to be sure they get to Nurnberg.'

'H'm. Farce, eh?'

'A showpiece for the Americans. A sop to the Russians – who should be on trial themselves.'

The dark, Welsh eyes studied him for a moment. The captain nodded briefly and left the chartroom. The midshipman, who had made himself small at the back of the room, came to the table.

'I'm glad, sir – you said you'd carry on.'

'Yes?'

'If the Pilot had been landed – he might have had to go to another ship.'

More likely to have been sent on sick leave until his ship returned, Reiss thought.

'You would prefer that he stayed with this one?'

'Yes sir. We get on quite well – and he teaches me a lot.'

'I like your loyalty. We'll see if we can increase your knowledge before he is back on duty, yes?'

'Yes, sir. Surprise him!'

Having a willing rather than sulking assistant made things more comfortable, particularly as the unfortunate Pilot's bout was severe and he was still wan and shaky when the ship tied

147

up in Piraeus. However, she was to remain in port for some seven days so he would be fit for the return voyage.

An hour later, Anstruther and Reiss were heading north, a bearded Greek at the wheel of a left-hand drive American jeep, driving them at reckless speed through ruined villages, along pot-holed roads. They were used to abandoning kit and had left the uniforms necessary for life on board in the ship and were wearing battledress with jerseys underneath and duffels on top and short leather sea boots.

They did not know who could give them the information they sought nor where they would find that person. Petros, the driver, was known to Anstruther and was prepared to take them wherever the trail led. The stop for that night was at a taverna in a village that consisted of that and little other than a single row of stone cottages.

There they fed handsomely on some sort of meat stew swimming in oil, followed by goat's milk cheese with olives and coarse bread and thick, sweet coffee. Their sleeping quarters consisted of a couple of mattresses beside the hearth where they rolled themselves in blankets over their clothes.

It was not until the third night that they got a name. They had settled into their parts, Anstruther as the quiet talking, polite Englishman – though a Scot – wheedling information and Reiss as the harsher spoken, more direct questioner. Together they began to elicit scraps of intelligence. The Greek Government had returned to Athens from Cairo in October of the previous year so they knew the executions must have taken place earlier, before the withdrawal of German units. But the exact date they did not know. It began to come clear as they pieced together individual memories. Then one of a group of three who had come to talk to them and admitted to have been partisan fighters under General Panos, spoke the magic words.

'It's Captain Andros you want to talk to,' he declared.

24

'Volos,' said Anstruther, stuffing his wash bag into the top of the haversack which they each carried for the minimum necessities. 'That's up on the East coast, isn't it?'

'About one hundred, one hundred-twenty kilometres,' agreed Reiss.

'H'm – two to three hours on these roads? Come on, then.'

Petros, on being consulted, confirmed that it would take up to three hours to reach the port of Volos on the East coast so they should be there before mid-day, weather and road conditions permitting.

'I hope to God they died quickly,' Anstruther muttered as the jeep set off. Hopefully nearing the end of the search, he was becoming more and more anxious about the fate of the SBS men. 'Any preferences for dying, Max?'

Reiss shrugged, smiling. 'In battle, a quick bullet rather than having one's legs blown off or your guts spilled,' he said. 'At home, perhaps one would like time to say goodbye. Wherever, I doubt if we shall have much say in the matter.'

Anstruther shot a quick look at him and smoothed his growing moustache.

'True,' he said and added jerkily, 'I think my brother drowned, slowly, trapped below deck. He'd got out of Greece, was being evacuated from Crete. Got on board Wryneck which was bombed and sunk. They say he was below...'

'I am sorry,' said Reiss, gently. He did not speak of Baldur though he had often wondered if the boy had been blown to pieces or injured and drowned like Anstruther's brother. 'So many deaths and to what end?'

149

'To a farce at Nurnberg, to millions of dollars of aid, to a threat from Russia,' growled Anstruther. 'No end.'

They settled to the journey. Both had lost brothers in 1941, both had seen out the war, relatively unscathed. Anstruther could only pray that such a world catastrophe would not occur in his son's lifetime; Reiss could only hope that somehow his country would rise again and find peaceful honour.

Volos was bitter. Some Greek gunboats were alongside the harbour walls and a few fishing boats at a further dockside. At anchor in the outer harbour lay a majestic cruiser. Reiss pulled binoculars from his haversack.

'British,' he said. 'Perhaps we can arrange a passage home.'

'Home, old son,' said Anstruther with a grin. 'Wouldn't you rather fly to Germany?'

He ducked the cuff aimed at him and added, 'Let's find Andros.'

A notice in Greek directed them to the Port captain's office and there they were received by a man in much braided and bemedalled Greek naval uniform. Andros's flab had developed into a firm bow-window and heavy jowls but he embraced his visitors with much goodwill and stood back to look at them – both duffel-coated, Anstruther in khaki battledress with a Marine beret and Reiss in naval battle dress and navy, gold peaked cap.

'How is my young Max?' he asked. 'Max, the Secret Serviceman with the SS written on his back!' He laughed heartily at his own cleverness.

'It's the other SS we're interested in, not the Secret Service,' said Anstruther. 'A unit here in Greece, probably just before the German forces pulled out. And a German intelligence officer who questioned a party of British commandos – prisoners of war – before handing them over to be executed.'

Andros, serious, sat down behind his desk, waving them to hard chairs.

'Prisoners of war, executed,' he repeated. 'Well, of course, it was done only too often, perhaps more often in the East than here.'

'Stop stalling, Niko,' said Reiss. 'Do you know anything?'

'Klaus Wengler headed the Intelligence section here at that time. Whether he conducted the questioning or not, I don't know. Most of the SS unit was destroyed in the withdrawal. Wengler got back to Germany. He would know.'

'Back where we started from,' sighed Anstruther. 'Can you tell us any more?'

'No,' said Andros with genuine regret. 'I do not know how or why they were executed. No doubt there will be records of it and they will turn up in the captured files. I cannot help you further.'

'Thank you for the information you have given us, Captain Andros.'

'You can help us in something else, Niko,' said Reiss. 'We are at a full stop here, sir?' Anstruther nodded and he went on. 'Can you signal the British cruiser to say we are here?'

'Aha! HMS *Monsarrat*, awaiting some members of the military mission! Yes, I can do that, Max.'

An exchange of signals, ship to shore, resulted in the final instruction: 'Colonel Anstruther and Commander Reiss to rejoin HMS *Monsarrat* and await further orders.'

So, after paying off and thanking Petros for his services, they went to the snow swept quayside to board the picket boat sent from the cruiser and endured a further fervent embrace from Captain Niko Andros who stood saluting as the very superior midshipman effortlessly manoeuvred away from the steps and set off across the harbour.

A long soak in a hot bath would have been welcome but they had just time to shower and change into fresh uniforms with shirt, tie and brass-buttoned tunic before presenting themselves for lunch in the wardroom.

'Glad you made it,' the Commander said in greeting. 'We're sailing at 1500 hours. At least, you won't have to be seeing to the Pilot's duties, Reiss. He's well recovered.'

That worthy, presenting a beaming face, confirmed his words and Reiss resigned himself to an idle voyage.

Orders came through while they were tied up to a rain-soaked quay in Gibraltar. *Monsarrat* was returning to her home port of Plymouth, Anstruther and Reiss to leave the ship there, Anstruther to fly to Hamburg and Reiss to report to London for dispersal procedure.

'A grateful country will give you a pat on the back and a reach-me-down suit and that'll be that,' said Anstruther with a grin. 'You should be back home for Christmas.'

'Come to Reissdorf for Christmas,' said Reiss, gazing at the whisky in his glass.

'If I don't get enough time to go to Edinburgh, I'll do just that. I'd like it.'

'It would help – my parents. Last time I was home for Christmas, Baldur was there.'

'The favourite son? Like my brother… Thanks. Unless they send me out of the country, I'll make it.

They travelled to London together where Anstruther departed from the RAF airfield to get a flight to Hamburg and Reiss took a taxi to the Admiralty. The 'temporary commission' had to come to an end he knew but could not deny that it was a wrench. It had happened to him before and he could accept it more easily than the abrupt curtailment of his previous life and career. The blank misery and despair that had engulfed him was still in his memory. This time was very different. His home was open to him, Pallant and Anstruther were in the country; he knew many members of the occupying forces, in Flensburg, in Kiel, in Hamburg, the Americans in Frankfurt and Coburg. And the prospect of a navy again before he was too old.

The demobilization procedure was brief and matter-of-fact. He had six weeks' leave and the clerical officer writing out the documents stopped in amazement when he gave his address.

As he came out he met Captain Hillman.

'I'm on the beach,' said Henry, ruefully. 'No further use for me. Oh, well, I'll return to my ancestral acres and join my father in idle retirement.'

It was cold, grey and miserable as only London could be on an early December day. Henry, who had joined the Navy like so many others for a lifetime career and was now a victim of post-war slashing of the Services, looked depressed, 'Join me for lunch,' said Reiss and Henry thankfully accepted. They took a short taxi ride to Jermyn Street and went to a discreet restaurant there behind the bombed St. James's Church, in Piccadilly.

'Toby's seventeen,' said Henry, sighing as he studied the menu. 'I wonder how long a career he can expect – if he ever gets posted to a ship.'

'I would suggest he specializes,' said Reiss. 'It is going to be a very technical service.'

'I'm sure you're right. And you? What about you?'

They paused to order. 'I am very fortunate. My father's marine engineering works is still in use. You could call him a war profiteer, I suppose. But the wounds he received have weakened him. He will be glad to have me there to help him deal with the Occupation.'

'You are indeed fortunate. But I think you are also regretful?'

'Of course. To lose one's profession twice!' Reiss glanced at the list the wine waiter offered and ordered briefly. Henry concealed a smile. The high-powered young lieutenant of the Hamburg café was not lost. Despite his three rings to Henry's four: but then, he had invited Henry to lunch.

Refreshed and restored, Henry caught his train to Exeter and there changed to the local that took him through Okehampton to Tavistock where Jean met him in the car. He found he was looking forward to a cup of tea by the fire.

'Well, it's Captain Hillman RN (Retired) now, I'm afraid,' he said. 'However, I met my ex-assistant Max Reiss and he gave me a splendid lunch. He's commander Reiss RNVR (Retired) now, I suppose – unless he's become ex-Kapitan-leutnant von Reissenburg!'

Manfred von Reissenburg or Max Reiss as he could remain for another six weeks, was considering his options. His travel warrant was made out to Hamburg but it didn't state how he was to get there. He had not bothered with the 'reach-me-down' clothes that Anstruther had mentioned so scathingly and felt he would not have too much luggage to cadge an air passage. But he had a need, a half-acknowledged desire to be fulfilled before he left England and abandoned his guise of a British naval officer. He took the train to Dover and there he struck lucky.

The following morning, in the dim, cold light of dawn, he paused to look around and remember. To remember the departures in *Mignonette* with the old general and the arrival in the stricken *Ditchling* with the dead on the bridge and the rescued soldiers cramming the decks and every space below.

'Commander Reiss, sir?' A cheerful voice broke in on his thoughts and a young two-and-a-half striper RNVR came up to him. 'You're coming with us to Hamburg, I'm told. I'm Hewer, CO.'

'Good morning, Captain. I was remembering – Dunkirk.'

'You were there? I was a snotty in a destroyer. Come aboard, sir. I'll send someone to pick up your bags.'

Hewer was CO of an MTB and senior officer of the small group of them who were proceeding that morning. He sent a seaman for Reiss's suitcase and holdall, invited his passenger to his diminutive bridge and embarked briskly on the business of getting under way. When they were safely out in the Channel, he handed over to his Number One and took Reiss down to breakfast.

25

By the end of the war these small, powerful boats – MTBs, MGBs, MLs – had been virtually taken over by the RNVR. An RN officer would perhaps be the senior officer of six or eight of them but his half-leader was usually RNVR. They were speedy, useful craft but as Hewer said over their breakfast coffee, they were all coming to the end of their time now and all bore the scars of combat and patching up.

'This is our last commission, I expect, sir. When they've finished with us in Hamburg we'll come back and be paid off. Then I'll have to find a job of some sort – I joined up from school so I've no qualifications.'

'They'll send you to university, I expect,' said Reiss.

'I hope so. I heard there was a scheme. Are you being posted to Hamburg, sir?'

'No.' Reiss remembered Henry Hillman's phrase. 'They've put me "on the beach". I'm going home.'

'Home, sir?' Hewer stared at him. 'I was in *Lindfield* in 1940. Our sister ship was *Ditchling*. Are you the foreign officer who brought her home?' His eyes dwelt on the ribbons revealed when Reiss had taken off his bridge coat. 'You got the DSC for it – Reiss – Max Reiss?'

Reiss nodded. 'How long ago it seems,' he murmured. The trip down the Thames was in his mind, the gathering of the little ships at Sheerness, the enormity of the whole operation. But Hewer was still seeking enlightenment.

'You live in Hamburg, sir? In Germany?'

'I was a naval officer but I found I could not serve Hitler.' If he said it many more times he would come to believe it himself. But how true was it? He had been proud to be an officer of the Kriegsmarine – he who was to be an Admiral like his father. But for his brush with Kranz and the Abwehr posting, presumably decided after his talk with Hillman had been reported, would he have gone on serving, would he have commerce-raided with *Graf Spee* or *Admiral Scheer*, made a dash through the Channel in *Scharnhorst* or *Gneisenau* – gone down in *Bismarck* with Baldur? As a naval officer he would not have known much about the camps, the atrocities, the shame that had brought his country to 'unconditional surrender' as demanded by Roosevelt and the total abolition of all its armed forces. So, in the end, had he survived, he would have been in much the same state as he was now, out of the service with just the hope that in ten or fifteen years time it might be revived and he could achieve his ambition and his father's flag rank.

He became aware of Hewer's regard and smiled, apologizing for his reverie. Hewer got up.

'I'd like to hear more, sir,' he said. 'I should say you've had a busy war. Please come up to the bridge when you wish to.' He picked up his duffel coat and cap and went out.

Reiss remained where he was and was shortly joined by the First Lieutenant, eager for his breakfast. He was about twenty-three and tucked into powdered eggs and tinned sausages with fried bread and cups of coffee with an appetite that took no notice of the tossing of the MTB as she met the turbulence of the North Sea.

'It was rotten luck the war ending so soon, sir,' he said, blithely and called the steward for toast and fresh coffee. 'I hoped to go east but the atom bombs put paid to that. I shall see if I can transfer to the regular navy.' He scraped butter on the toast and spread marmalade lavishly. The Skipper says you're on demob leave, sir. What's it like – or do you want to be out?'

'No.' Reiss was amused by the youngster's brashness. 'I feel – bereft.'

'The Navy's your father and mother?' Number One grinned. 'You're an orphan, sir! I'd feel like that. I was in the

156

Sea Cadets at school and came into the Navy as a CW candidate then I went to King Alfred. Were you at Hove, sir?'

'No. Greenwich.' Reiss got up, he decided to take advantage of he Skipper's invitation and sought permission to go up to the bridge.

The CO grinned, 'Number One driven you out, sir? He's a great talker. Bright lad, though.'

Reiss propped himself in a corner out of the way. The bridge was already occupied by the CO, the sub-lieutenant, helmsman and signalman but this, he accepted sadly, was likely to be his last sea voyage for the foreseeable future and he did not want to spend it all below. The wind was keen and there was sleet and icy spray in it. He pulled the collar of his bridge coat about his ears and let the throb of the engines, the sound of wind and wave, the terse exchanges between the watch keepers, all flow over him and keep pace with his thoughts.

Lunch was served at 1230 hours and taken by Reiss, the Skipper and the Sub., Number One and the Snotty being on the bridge. Tinned stew with tinned mashed potato was followed by tinned rice pudding with a dollop of plum jam. Over coffee, Reiss managed to keep his companions amused with tales of meals eaten with the partisans in Greece and in the fisherman's cottage in Malta. He was aware that Hewer had many questions on his mind and when the Sub. left them, he waited to see what came.

'Sir, you are going back to Germany, having spent the war on the other side,' said Hewer, carefully. 'How do you expect to be received?'

'Some may think I should be shot,' said Reiss. 'But, of course, there are no Nazis now and everyone is working for the British and Americans. So I shall not be out of place.' He saw Hewer accept the cynicism. 'And I have been back, collecting material for the Nurnberg trials.'

Hewer made a slight movement of distaste.

'How could you do that, sir?'

'I could not. So they sent me to Greece again. And now I am of no further use.'

'I am sorry.' But he was still plainly unhappy.

'I cannot make you understand,' said Reiss, quietly. 'The punishments, the reprisals, for anyone who opposed Hitler, the threats to one's family.'

'So how did you keep yours safe?'

How? By being missing, presumed dead? By supplying carefully filtered information and gaining promotion and a medal for work amongst the enemy? Because his father was serving in the Navy and his brother died in the Bismarck? By sinking a U-boat, by shooting Kranz, by tracking down Klaus Wengler? He put a hand to his eyes and shook his head. It was a question he could not answer and, after a moment, Hewer got up and went quietly from the wardroom.

It had been dark for some time when they passed Cuxhaven and entered the estuary of the Elbe. Reiss requested permission to go to the bridge again and watched their steady progress up river. Hewer had made a quiet apology.

'I'm sorry, sir. I shouldn't have pushed you so far.'

'Please, Captain. My family was safe.'

They had left it at that. A rude shout from a passing tugboat in German prompted Hewer to hand the loud hailer to Reiss and ask him to reply in a suitable manner. The tug master was silenced.

Reiss had already requested that a signal might be made to the Base to see if Colonel Anstruther RM was there and the reply arrived as they were dining. The cook had made a great effort and produced spam fritters and tinned tomatoes, followed by tinned jam sponge pudding and custard. The signalman brought in the message as they started on the coffee. Hewer read it with a grin. 'Colonel Anstruther requests permission to board you with ouzo on arrival. What's ouzo, sir?'

'I'm afraid it is a request for a party. But he is a Scotsman. He'll bring whisky not ouzo which is Greek.'

'Well! Farewell party, sir. Good show.'

They tied up an hour later and Hewer went ashore to report their arrival. He returned with Anstruther, a couple of bottles in his greatcoat pockets and clutching another. With them came the CO and the Sub. from the companion boat. Most of the crews had gone to shore quarters leaving only a small guard on board.

'We'll just welcome these fellows to their stint in Hamburg as it will keep them over Christmas,' said Anstruther, cheerfully. 'Then we'll get back to the Base – you'll be my guest for the night, Max.'

The party – whether a welcome or a farewell – went with a swing.

'You've done quite a bit with the Commander, sir?' Hewer asked Anstruther.

'Yes. He's done a lot for us.'

'But what has it done to him?'

Anstruther took a pull at his glass.

'You mean working against his own country? His stance has always been that he wanted to free Germany from the Nazis. I think he took one of the better ways to do that.'

'And now?'

'And now he's got to help build it up again. Come on. Give me another whisky and then we'll be off.'

The following day was Christmas Eve: Heiliger Abend, the principal day of a German Christmastide. While Anstruther 'cleared his desk' in preparation for his absence, Reiss went out to look at he ruined seaport. Heavy air-raids had caused mass destruction. The docks and river had first call on the clearance work and, as Reiss knew both from departure in *Monsarrat* and arrival in the MTB, great strides had been made. But the actual town near to the docks was not yet showing signs of rehabilitation.

War crimes trials were to be held here too so both American and Russian delegates with attendant troops, were present as well as the British in whose zone it was. Remembering the nights of raging fires and the streets of shattered buildings that he had witnessed in London, in Portsmouth, Liverpool and Plymouth, Reiss could not find greater horror here than he had felt there. A sense of futility, of waste, of despair at the monstrous stupidity of man assailed him. For what had so many died?

He recognized the café where he had first met Captain Hillman with the American Parkin. It was a ruined shell. But here he had spoken the words that had changed his life and that was why men had died: to stop Hitler and the Nazis from conquering Europe. Perhaps he had done the right thing after all – even if not entirely of his own volition.

Anstruther had drawn a car from the pool and after lunch in the British Officers' quarters, they stowed their baggage in the boot and Anstruther laid a bouquet of winter foliage and blossom carefully on the back seat with a box of American chocolates.

'Hope your Mama will like them,' he observed. 'And Papa drinks Scotch?'

'And Scots are supposed to be close-fisted?' said Reiss.

'Well – you're saving me three days' mess bills,' retorted Anstruther. 'Then I'm off home for the New Year. We celebrate Hogmanay in Scotland more than Christmas. An awful irreligious lot we are.'

'You will be expected to attend church tomorrow,' said Reiss, straight-faced. Then, more seriously, 'I hope you are not giving up time at home because I asked you to come to mine?'

'Well, I am, old son but only because I want to.' Anstruther smoothed his fairly trim moustache and inserted his lean length into the driver's seat. 'Truth to tell,' he went on as Reiss joined him 'Christmas in Scotland is bloody dull and once I've see Janet and Fergus, I get bored to tears. A week at home is long enough for me.'

The sentry at the gate stopped them and a Petty Officer with white belt and gaiters peered in at them.

'You did oughta 'ave a German driver, sir,' he said. 'You know – if you have a h'accident, they get the blame!'

'Yes, I know that one,' said Anstruther, brightly. 'Actually, I've got a German driver but he's not driving.' He flipped a hand to his beret in reply to the RPO's salute and drove on.

Anstruther did not refer again to his inability to cope with long leave until that evening. They had passed the journey in casual conversation and a lively appreciation of the countryside and of the mainly destroyed towns through which they passed. A pause in Reissbaden to 'make their number' with Major Bailey and they went on up to Reissdorf. The – relatively – small schloss raised Anstruther's eyebrows and he got out of the car and gazed at its facade with admiration.

The elderly Josef, whose active service had been confined to the Great War and a young footman, Karl, who had been a U-boat crewman, came down the steps to meet them and Karl took the car and their baggage to the nether regions while Josef followed them into the hall, bearing the bouquet.

There, Manfred von Reissenburg greeted his mother, kissing her hand and then her cheek and presented his companion.

'I shall look forward to hearing of some of your Greek adventures, colonel,' she said.

'And I shall enjoy telling you of them, Ma'am,' he said.

The Admiral, shaking hands, added 'We hear little of them from Manfred.'

'Oh, he's a modest lad,' said Anstruther which made the admiral look surprised.

Later, before dinner, Anstruther, bathed and refreshed, sought the man he knew as Max Reiss in his apartments.

'Still in your uniform,' he remarked. 'Keeps me company, anyway.'

'I have nothing else,' said Reiss. 'Come.' He went into his dressing-room and pulled open the doors of a floor-length wardrobe. Anstruther gazed at a complete set of Kriegsmarine uniforms, greatcoat, bridge coats, reefers, dress uniforms, mess kit, tropical whites, still with the two rings and star of a leutnant zur see and greatcoat, raincoat, bridge coats, reefers and whites with the RNVR three rings and curl and on the floor naval type shoes, black and white, leather sea boots – and the sandy desert boots. And at one end, a pre-war civilian lounge suit plus evening kit, tails and dinner jacket and a hacking jacket.

'Yes,' said Anstruther. 'Not much choice, I see.' On a shelf he saw the medals in their cases, the DSO, DSC and bar, the service medals and – the Iron Cross. Also plain and gold peaked caps of either service.

'There is my past,' said Reiss. 'What is the future?'

They went back into the sitting-room and Reiss poured out a couple of schooners of the Admiral's fine, dry sherry. Anstruther, relaxing in a deep armchair, took an appreciative sip and raised eyes, suddenly bleak.

'It worries me, Max,' he said. 'I am terrified of the axe. They dumped you because you balked at the Nurnberg documents. What will they use me for, now? If they chuck me out, I shall probably go and lose myself on a Greek mountain.'

'And Janet and the boy?'

'Get on perfectly well without me. She'll have a widow's pension and he'll get reduced fees at a school for the sons of naval officers.' He sipped some more sherry. 'I'm over forty, Max. Not much of a chance in Civvy Street.'

'You must have thought of retirement.'

'No. I didn't expect to come through. You should have let me drown in the Med.'

Reiss got up from the deep window seat and took Anstruther's glass.

'I would have lost my medal,' he pointed out, smiling. 'Come on. My father will want you to have a drink with him before dinner.'

They went downstairs. The Christmas tree with its lights was in the corner by the stone hearth, the log fire blazed. Anstruther's bouquet with the colourful foliage and bright blossoms was arranged in a tall vase on a table, beside a photograph of Baldur in his cadet uniform, his young face laughing, and his eyes keen and bright. To the other side was one of his more austere older brother in German naval uniform, gazing out a little disdainfully. On the wall a portrait of the admiral in the uniform of a Captain in the Imperial Navy, long coat and wing collar. Companion to that, his wife, the Grafin, as a young woman. Their surviving son, in a well-worn uniform of the British Naval Reserve, took her in to dinner, placing her chair for her and putting Anstruther on her right.

True to his promise, the colonel related tales of the Greek excursions with some enjoyment, picking the amusing, the amazing and the slightly hairy parts of their adventures.

'You should have seen Max tucking into goat stew, Ma'am,' he said. 'And as for ouzo and retsina – but there was nothing to beat whisky at night in the mountains, eh, Max?'

'I have evidently not been fully appreciative of my son's versatility,' remarked the Admiral. 'And I have always found him quite abstemious.'

'On duty yes, sir. In fact, he asked for Evian water in the wardroom once when he might have had to take our ship into Wilhelmshaven. The Pilot was taken ill and Max stood in for him.'

The Admiral regarded his son who was continuing to enjoy his dinner while listening with some amusement to Anstruther's tales.

'Manfred, I see you in a new light,' his father teased him.

'Yes, sir. A better one, I trust.' Reiss was also amused to see that his mother was more than taken with the Scotsman. They were hitting it off very well and her avid interest was making him exert his powers of narration. His love and knowledge of Greece was very evident and Reiss wondered if that was where he would finish his days.

For church on Christmas Day, Anstruther replaced his marine beret with the peaked cap with its scarlet band and the globe badge showing the Eastern Hemisphere. He was proud of his uniform and appreciated the respectful interest in it accorded him by Reissdorf's villagers. That all of them had not yet accepted the role played by Graf Reissenburg's elder son, he discovered next day.

They had spent the afternoon of Christmas Day touring as much of the estate as they could on foot and in company with the Admiral. Anstruther had brought a tweed suit and thick jersey with him and Reiss had changed into much the same with his riding jacket, cords and desert boots. One of the cottages had the American Forces Network on the wireless and the strident sound of a brass band stomping out the Battle Hymn of the Republic followed them along the lane.

'I am glad we are in the British zone,' said the Admiral reflectively. 'I have always got on well with the British. You told me, Manfred, you had met Henry Hillman and his father with whom I was acquainted at the end of the last war.'

'Yes sir.'

'We should never – never have gone to war with them again. Hitler did not intend to, of course.'

He was happy talking with them, because he rarely had a Service audience except when he had occasion to meet with Major Bailey or his deputy. He was still an Imperialist at heart; Anstruther decided and had little good to say either of the Weimar republic or the Third Reich. He was fatalistic about what form of constitution would come next.

Coming downstairs that evening, after bathing and changing back into uniform for dinner, Anstruther heard what was obviously an altercation between Josef and Karl, albeit in hushed tones. They were making up the fires and ceased their talk immediately on seeing the Marine Colonel. He wondered idly how the elderly man, ex-Imperial Fleet like his master and the young ex-U-boatman, a local youth who had been at Lorient, could ever agree.

Reiss walked into the result of that altercation the following morning, obeying a summons from his father.

'Josef has been to see me,' said the Admiral, directly. 'He tells me that Karl says you were sent to England by the Abwehr and supplied information to them and to Himmler's SD throughout the war. That on their instructions you got appointed to Plymouth to report on invasion preparations. That in Greece, you made contact with Colonel SS Kranz and reported to him. Some of this you and Commodore Pallant spoke of during his visit. I was willing to accept your defection to England as an anti-Nazi but I cannot accept this sort of double-crossing. Is it true?'

'How would Karl know of it?'

'He had a cousin in the SD.'

Reiss half-turned away. He saw that Anstruther had stopped rigidly in the act of entering the room and signed to him to come in. How best to explain to his father the humiliation of the SS beatings, the despair over his wrecked career and banishment from home, the resignation of the Jews in the refugee ship, the awful thrill, fear and wonderment of the little ships at Dunkirk? He saw the Admiral notice and accept Anstruther's presence. He faced his father again.

'I told you the Abwehr sent me,' he said, quietly. 'I told you of the refugee Jews and that I gave myself up to the British Naval Intelligence people. I went to Dunkirk with a gallant old man to rescue Allied troops. I cannot describe to you the effect that had on me. I accepted a temporary commission in the British navy reserve and I was proud to be one of them. I was on duty in a British corvette when we engaged and sank a U-boat. I went to Greece and met Kranz three times and killed him because I thought he was beginning to suspect me. I went to Plymouth and assisted in the preparations to invade Normandy and helped to rescue American troops who were being shot up by E-boats. Every piece of information I passed to my contacts was given to me by Commodore Pallant. Yes, I betrayed the Third Reich. I gave my allegiance to England and I never betrayed them.'

For a long moment father and son faced one another. Then the Admiral looked at Anstruther. 'Colonel, this is true?' he asked.

'Entirely. He has left out the bit where he saved my life after our boat was bombed and sunk in the Mediterranean. But you must understand, sir, what the rejection of his country – or of the rulers of his country – has meant to him. It is a desperately hard thing to do. It leaves scars.'

'Yes, I can understand.' The Admiral gripped Reiss's upper arms, looking into his face. 'You are my son,' he said. 'And I love you.' He went from the room.

Reiss went to a side table. 'Gin or sherry?' he asked.

'I think gin this time,' said Anstruther. 'What brought this up?'

'Karl had a cousin in Himmler's intelligence section.'

'I heard him arguing with Josef last night. Will you have him sacked?'

'No. He needs the job.' Reiss swallowed his gin. 'What I have done is done. I can't undo it and I don't regret it. But – if I let them believe I was a double agent then I was working for the Nazis. If I let them know the truth, in their eyes I am a traitor. What do I do?'

'Be like Brer Rabbit – lie low and say nuffin.' Anstruther laughed. 'They'll work it out for themselves and believe what it suits them to believe. In the meantime, you become boss man at the factory, is that it?'

Manfred von Reissenburg, nearing the end of his impersonation of Max Reiss, drew a deep sight.

'That is it,' he said. 'But, Hugh –'

'Yes, old son?'

'If you ever decide to go to that Greek mountain, call in for me, will you?'

Anstruther eyed him, considering. He recalled the Admiral's barely concealed relief and renewed pride when he had confirmed Reiss's account of his defection. He visualized the colossal task waiting in the aftermath of this war. He saw himself looking upon Fergus with the eyes of a father whose belief in his son's honour remains.

'I think we shall both be too busy to go wandering on a Greek mountain,' he said. 'But when we've cleared this lot up, come and join me on a Scottish one, for a change.'